Bridges Into the Imagination #3

M. R. Williamson

Bridges Into the Imagination Book 3
by M. R. Williamson

Cover art and design by Marcia A. Borell

First Printing, October 2022

Hiraeth Publishing
P.O. Box 1248
Tularosa, NM 88352

e-mail: hiraethsubs@yahoo.com

This anthology is dedicated to my wife, Connie Louise Gordin Williamson. Without her understanding and encouragement, I would have still been a poet today.

Pragamore Chronicles
Creating friends and fans,
one reader at a time.

Introduction

In the everlasting tradition of Speculative Fiction, I submit to you this third edition on 'Bridges Into the Imagination'. This collection of my best Short Stories will hold your attention from beginning to end. Keep reading and I'll keep writing. . .

M. R. Williamson

Contents

First Offering:
Cry Wolf

A late evening breeze drifted softly across the gravel road as Ray Laxton sat on his front porch. Enjoying the scent of the woods, the old farmer closed his eyes and for the first time in a great while, was finally tempted to daydream. Just as the eighty-year-old started to drift away, the sharp bang of the screen door severely diminished that capacity. Glancing a bit to his right, he caught the eager expression of a much younger person--his granddaughter, Shelley Cullum. The ten-year-old pulled an old fold-up chair over next to him, sat down, but said not a word.

"And you want . . ." started Ray, closing his eyes again.

"Spin us a story, Gramps," she responded. Moving her chair a bit more in front of the old fellow, she added, "Not just any old story though. Grandma said you knew one about an Indian boy and a dog, back when you worked on the Mississippi with Gabby."

"Great Lands," managed Ray. He wiped his eyes with his red bandanna and slowly looked back at the young girl. "You sure made the cobwebs fly with that one, Pumpkin."

"You were there, right?" Shelley's eyes widened.

Of all the people west of the Mississippi, she knew her grandfather was the best storyteller. That was mainly because he had lived the ones he told.

"There?" Ray's old blue eyes sparkled as he pulled his old briar pipe from his overalls and then searched for his pouch. Finding it in his back pocket this time, he took it out, unzipped it, and then looked back at his granddaughter. "Of course I was, Pumpkin. It all happened right inside this old, clapboard house. He wasn't even as old as you are--about six I would guess."

"The straight skinny now Gramps. Don't frill it up,"

quipped Shelley, watching him intently.

"Well . . ." Ray carefully stoked his old pipe, struck a sulfur-tipped match on the back leg of his coveralls. and then added, "Now-a-days that 'straight' stuff is just about impossible to get, but I'll try nonetheless. You see, these days, you've got movies about werewolves as big as horses and strange people who sparkle in the sunlight." He then leaned back and blew out a perfect circle of smoke. "Rubbish," was the word he added behind the circle. Looking back at his granddaughter, he continued, "Then, as if that's not enough, some young teenager comes along and changes, quick as a cat's sneeze, into a blood-sucking demon with teeth sharperin' your grandmother's ice pick. More rubbish," he quipped.

As he rested his head on the back of his chair, returned his gaze to the woods beyond the gravel road, and then continued.

"Charlie Youngblood didn't climb trees faster'n a squirrel, run faster'n a deer, nor did he have the talents of Bat Man."

Shelley squinted her eyes, gathered her long, brown hair to her right shoulder, and then asked, "Doesn't that kind of take the punch out of the story?"

The old steamboat veteran smiled. "Bless her heart. If your Grandmother Margaret were here right now, she'd say that sometimes the truth is much more scarier than fiction. Anyways, me and old Gabby Hollis--I was much younger at the time--had just got off the River Queen at Richardson Landing, just south of Memphis. It was a Friday evening, we had the whole weekend off, and . . . ."

* * *

Gabby scratched his four-inch, bushy beard listening to the boards creek on the gangplank as he and Ray walked from the River Queen. "Not 'nuf nails," he grumbled. "If this new gangplank comes apart and dumps us, I'm gonna find me one of those boards and--"

"Three men worked on this thing not long ago, Gabby," interrupted Ray.

"Well . . ." started the old fellow. He looked back squinty-eyed at Ray and then added, "You're gonna help me out tha water ain't ya?"

Ray laughed silently as he replied, "If I make it out of the water."

Once across the gangplank, the two headed across the gravel parking lot toward Ray's old fifty Chevy.

"I'm so proud to see March I could shout," quipped Gabby. He exhaled heavily and then watched his breath swirl in the slight breeze. I thought nineteen fifty-eight was cold, but its icy remnants have just about froze my britches off."

The old character, clearly in his seventies, was still remarkably spry, though time had put a catch in his right leg.

"Well, it's still cold. March hasn't warmed February up a bit. And stop scratching your whiskers," grumbled Ray as he scratched his head. "You've got me itchin' all over. Why don't you just shave that thing off?"

"Nope," quipped Gabby as he smoothed his gray whiskers back to his chin. "Wouldn't look like me if'n I did. Besides, my old bull dog wouldn't let me out of tha car."

Ray chuckled as he fumbled with his keys. Upon finding the one to his Chevy, he said, "Margaret's made a big pot of beef stew. I know it's well after 7:00pm, but I'll bet she'll fix us a big pone of yeller cornbread if you'll stay the night with us. There's nothin' warm at your house except that old bulldog."

Gabby walked to the far side of the car, opened the door, and then got in. "That big couch by the fire does sound temptin' though. Think she'll mind?"

"You're her only uncle, Gabby. She'd be tickled."

"Good," replied the old fellow through a broad grin. "It'll be the first time in almost a month that I'll be able to sleep in somethin' that doesn't move one way or ta' other"

Ray started the Chevy, eased off on the clutch, and the old car lurched forward. Two more gears and they were lumbering east on the Richardson Landing Road and away from the paddle wheeler. They had barely turned south on Old Drummonds Road when Gabby quickly sat up.

Slow down a bit, Ray," he requested as he pushed his black, horn-rimmed glasses closer to his nose. "There's somethin' up ahead a ways. I saw its eyes shine in the lights."

Just as Ray pressed the bright light button on the floorboard, something darted from the scrub on the left and darted through the beams of their lights.

"Geeeze!" exclaimed Ray as he slammed on the brakes, bringing the Chevy to a sliding stop. "What the devil was that?" he added excitedly.

Gabby, pushing himself away from the dash, exclaimed, "I don't believe my eyes." Quickly opening the door, the old riverboat man got out, looked up ahead in the lights, and then back to the hogweed just right of the Chevy. "This one don't belong to the eyes I saw, Ray. What we almost hit was a young boy, and a naked one to boot."

Ray quickly got out and walked around to the front of the car. He then slowed and approached the shoulder of the gravel road like he expected a deer to run out of the hogweed at any moment. "Naked, did you say?" he asked as he peered through the eight foot hogweed and Johnson grass.

"Well, you usually are when you don't have anythin' on. Look for 'em right about there, Ray," said the old fellow as he pointed toward a part in the weeds. Walking back out in front of the Chevy, he added, "The eyes I saw in the lights was a big dog, I believe. He's probably still a little ways up ahead."

"You're right about where the boy went in, Gabby," agreed Ray still peering into the weeds.

"Careful," warned Gabby, watching Ray kneel down on the gravel for a better look.

"Sweet Jesus on the cross," whispered Ray. "It is a boy and he looks wilder'n a March hare."

Gabby turned, pushed his heavy, black, horn-rimmed glasses back upon his nose, and then eased up behind Ray.

Wide-eyed and bare beamed, the youngster stared back at them as his breath fogged up the air in his little, would be 'hideout'. Looking about six years old, his coal black hair was at his shoulders and impregnated with beg-a-lice, grass, and cocklebururs. Although scratched up a bit, his tanned skin didn't look badly damaged.

"Get on the far side of the car, Gabby," suggested Ray. "We don't want to scare him. Let's see if I can coax him out and into the Chevy."

"Very well," responded Gabby reluctantly as he slowly backed away.

Noting that the boy immediately shook his head, Ray laughed and said, "Well, at least you understood me." Taking off his jacket, he added, "Cold and hungry I'll bet. You can put on my jacket right now. I'll take you to a warm place and get you somethin' hot to eat. Would you like that?"

"Watch out for the big, black dog," warned the boy as he leaned forward for a better look up the road. His words were soft but he still looked to be satisfied with where he was at the present. Then, as he eyed the quilted jacket, he added, "It was on the road when you came up."

"I'll check," said Gabby, "You watch the boy."

After retrieving a flashlight from the Chevy's glove compartment, the old riverboat man walked out in front of the car and searched the woods.

"Wait a second," he finally said, directing the light's beam to just in front of where he was standing. "There's somethin' here in the sand. It's his tracks and he's a big 'un."

"Big what?" asked Ray, watching the lad's eyes grow big.

"They're oval tracks—not a bit round like a dog or even a hound."

"Wolf?" asked Ray, just above a whisper.

Gabby slowly nodded. Now, with a renewed interest in the woods and scrub near him, he slowly backed toward the driver's door, opened it, and then suggested, "I'd get in the car right now boys, if I were you."

Ray slowly backed up and then opened the passenger side door.

Glancing back at Gabby, he whispered, "You drive." Looking back to the boy, he said, "We believe you, son. My friend's found his tracks. Please come with us. The beast is probably watching us right now."

The boy then dashed out of the weeds, slipped into the jacket, and then climbed into the front seat beside Gabby.

"What's your name, son?" asked Gabby as he cranked the old Chevy.

Hugging the coat close to him, the boy slowly looked up. "Youngblood," he said weakly, and then looked to the weeds on the left side of the road.

"Got a first name?" quipped Gabby.

"Youngblood," the lad repeated.

"I see. "What happened to your clothes?" asked Gabby.

"Lost 'em," answered the boy, just above a whisper.

Twenty minutes later, Gabby slowed and then pulled into the Laxton driveway. It was well after 8:00pm but the lights were still on as well as the one on the porch.

* * *

Meanwhile, inside the Laxton home, their eighteen-year-old daughter, Susan, sat in the recliner near the fire, reading her short story anthology, 'Clockwork Spells and Magical Bells'. She quickly noticed the Chevy's lights as it pulled into the drive.

"Mom! Dad's home!" she exclaimed as she jumped from the chair and ran to the front door. "Gabby's with him, and . . ." Her voice trailed off as she noticed the young boy step out behind her father.

"I've got the stew heating," replied Margaret. "Now what's this about 'and'?" The thirty-eight-year-old housewife stood in the kitchen doorway watching Susan peering through the window. Wiping her hands on her apron, she repeated, "And what, young lady?"

"There's a child with them, mother--a young boy. I think." explained Susan as she opened the screen door.

While Susan held the door open, Margaret slowly walked into the living room. "Child?" she echoed, trying to get a glimpse through the door as she drew close.

"We've got company, Margaret," announced Ray. As he hugged his daughter, he then added, "and I'm not talking about your uncle."

"I see we do," noted Margaret, in all but a whisper. "Well, come inside and shut the door. We'll be chasin' butterflies all night if you don't."

"There moths, Mom," corrected Susan.

"Whatever," laughed Margaret.

"We have no idea who he is," explained Ray. "Gabby and I found him on the Old Drummonds Road, not far from the dock." He looked at Susan. "Do me and Youngblood here a favor and look in my closet. Surely there's somethin' he can wear for tonight."

"He looks scared to death and scratched all over," noted Susan as she left for her parent's bedroom.

"We'll fix that," replied Margaret. Holding out her hand toward the boy, she added, "Come, sweetie. I'll draw you a nice, hot bath and get those beg-a-lice and cockle burrs out of your hair."

The boy watched her intently on the way to the bathroom. Something about the lady seemed to calm him. Perhaps it was her turquoise, print dress, or her burgundy blouse. Maybe it was her white, thunderbird necklace. At any rate, he went straight to her and never looked back at all.

"What's your name, dear?" asked Margaret. She turned on the faucets to the tub.

"Charlie Youngblood . . . Shoshone," finally responded the boy as Margaret adjusted the hot water flowing into the tub.

"Don't bite your nails, dear. There's nothing to fear here," assured Margaret. As she examined his hands, she added, "You've got them almost to the quick. Now let's have that jacket. You can't take a bath with it on. I'll draw the drapes for you."

Reluctantly, the six-year-old removed the jacket and slipped quickly behind the drapes.

"Ohhh my," replied Margaret weakly as she rummaged through the medicine cabinet. "You're gonna look like you're on the war--" Margaret paused, smiled at the boy, and then said, "I guess I could just dip you in alcohol, but it would take Susan to catch you if I did." She then took a little bottle of Mercurochrome from the medicine cabinet, held it up to the light, and then shook it. "We'll use this, sweetie," she said, smiling toward the boy. "It won't sting like the other. Margaret stepped from the bathroom and eased the door closed. "I've got him started. The cornbread should be almost dun when he gets through." Turning toward her daughter, she added, "Susan, go to the linen closet and get sheets, blankets, and pillows for our guests. We'll put the boy on the small couch next to the television and Gabby on the larger one next to the fireplace."

"That'll be just fine, Margaret," assured Gabby. "That stew and cornbread certainly smells good."

"Thank you. I'll have it on the table when Charlie finishes."

"Charlie?" queried Gabby. "We couldn't get anythin' but Youngblood."

"Takes a woman's touch, old man," quipped Susan from the other side of the house.

"Old man?" Gabby rolled his eyes, scratched his beard, and then pushed his glasses back on his nose.

* * *

About an hour later, the Shoshone boy sat cross-legged in front of the hearth, eating his stew and watching the fireplace. Other than the occasional stare at Susan's long, brown hair, or to check and see where Margaret was, he never moved from his spot.

After finishing, Susan got up and peeped at him from the dining room doorway. "Want some more stew?" she asked.

Charlie nodded, pulling the oversized, flannel shirt closer to his neck.

"Have the dogs been fed?" asked Ray as he began collecting the leftovers.

Charlie immediately stopped eating and looked to his left, toward one of the front windows.

"Just give it to Bear," suggested Susan. "I've already fed the coonhounds and hosed out their pens."

"You're a treasure," replied Ray. "I'll just--"

With that, Charlie dropped his spoon to the hearth and sprang to his feet. "Bring the dogs in!" he exclaimed. "The big, black one will surely kill them if you don't."

Susan froze just inside the living room with Charlie's second bowl of stew in hand. "What's he talking about, Father," she asked as Charlie's words also brought

Margaret from the kitchen as well.

"He looks scared to death," noted Margaret.

"Everybody just take a deep breath," suggested Gabby as he stood from his chair at the table. "When we found him, he said a big dog was chasin' him. I don't think he was lyin' 'cause I saw its tracks in the gravel."

"Awww, Gabby," complained Ray. "That was a good ways from here. I don't think the animal could keep up with us. We were doing over forty on the Old Drummonds Road."

Youngblood then ran straight to Margaret, grabbed her about the waist, and then exclaimed, "He'll find me! He'll find me! Please, put the dogs inside."

"Calm down, son," said Margaret softly as she examined his hands. "You've been biting your nails again. They're almost bleeding. The hounds are in a heavy wire, fenced pen with a concrete bottom. They're safe enough. Bear doesn't like it in here, besides, he's a white mastiff and as big as a horse. No animal in his right mind would dare jump on him. Now, go and sit back down by the hearth. Susan has your stew and cornbread."

Pulling back from her a bit, Charlie's expression seemed to be laced with not only fear, but a bit of sorrow. Reluctantly, the young fellow went back to the fireplace and then looked back at Susan.

"Right here," responded Susan as she brought another bowl of stew with a slice of cornbread wrapped in a paper napkin.

He then looked up at her. "Is the big dog outside yours?" he asked just above a whisper.

"He is, sweetie," she answered, "but don't worry, Bear is very vocal if anything strange gets close. If it comes, I'll go and chase it away."

"No! No!" he exclaimed, almost in horror. Dropping his spoon back into the bowl he quickly jumped to his feet again. "You still don't understand. He IS here! He watches, even now! Don't go out in the dark!"

Susan hugged the child and then looked up at her mother. "He's crying," she said softly.

"All right. All right, son," replied Ray as he took the

double barrel, twelve gauge Bellmore from over the fireplace.

Checking it as he walked to the door, he paused to peep through the window. He then opened it, and stepped onto the front porch. With his breath showing in the air, he replied, "Bear's right here by me." Looking out into the dark of the woods across the gravel road, he quipped, "If he was any more relaxed, he'd be dead."

Gabby eased up beside him, looked out toward Black Bottoms also, and then softly added, "We've coyotes, bobcats, and even the occasional panther, but never have I ever seen a wolf, especially one larger than that white Mastiff."

Ray glanced at Bear, and then looked back at Gabby. "Are you sure of this?" he whispered.

Gabby nodded and then whispered, "Oval, and as big as my palm," he answered softly. "If he comes, he'll give Susan's dog a run for his money. Perhaps you might best put him in, at least until we get a handle on this."

"He'll keep us up all night, howling and scratching to get out," said Ray. "Besides, he'll let us know if something is out there." He then handed Gabby the double and added, "Put the Bellmore by the couch. I've got the Smithy in the nightstand."

"You two are spooked, aren't you?" asked Susan, pausing behind them at the doorway. "All this whispering is making me nervous."

Turning with a bit of a smile, Ray explained, "The coon hounds couldn't be quieter." Then, nodding toward the Mastiff, he added, "Bear's fast asleep."

Susan nodded, stepped away from the doorway, and then looked at Charlie. He was still slowly eating his stew, but had turned away from the fireplace and was now looking past the coffee table and out of the window behind Gabby's couch.

"What now?" asked Gabby as the two walked back into the living room.

"It's almost 10:00pm," replied Ray through a long yawn. "You two can watch television, but I'm tuckered out. Susan will be reading in her room for a bit. I'm sure you and the boy will have the room to yourselves."

"That's me also," replied the old riverboat man as he watched Margaret and Susan bring in the blankets, sheets, and pillows.

* * *

Late that night, Gabby lay fast asleep on the huge, leather couch near the fireplace. With its embers still glowing, they were doing their job a bit too well for the old fellow. He had already pushed his blanket down. The extra heat had kept his mind spinning and now the motion of his imaginary paddle wheeler was, once again, gently moving him back and forth. He was just about to get out of his bunk when a high-pitched scream ripped through the silence.

"All hands on deck! All hands on deck!" he shouted as he rolled off the couch and onto the hardwood floor.

With Ray's coonhounds howling in the background, Gabby quickly scrambled to his feet, took a quick step toward the dining room, and then promptly tumbled over the coffee table. Recovering a bit slower than usual, he heard another scream come rolling down through the dining area again. Still on his hands and knees, he scrambled to where he could see through the dining room and on to the hallway toward the back door.

That came from outside, he thought, seeing the back door wide open.

"What the devil was that?" asked Ray as he stepped into the hallway in his boxers.

"It came from outside, father," answered Susan. With a firm grip on her door, she looked almost afraid to step into the hallway.

"Take this," suggested Margaret, handing Ray his housecoat.

"What's happening?" asked Gabby. But as he stood, he saw the fuzzy, pitch-black silhouette of an animal trot by the back door to the west side of the house, and it wasn't Bear. "My glasses!" he exclaimed. Then, as he turned back to the coffee table, he said loudly, "The wolf's here, Ray! He's on the west side of the house!"

"Get the Bellmore, Gabby!" shouted Ray as he wheeled and all but carried Margaret back into their bedroom.

Grabbing his glasses from the table, Gabby put them on with one hand and grabbed the shotgun leaning against the wall with the other. Quickly turning from the couch, his gaze fell upon the smaller couch on the far side of the front door.

"The boy's gone, Ray, and the back door's wide open!" he exclaimed as he rushed toward the dining room.

As he entered the dining room, the old riverboat man caught a clear glimpse of another animal. But it only offered a glimpse of white as it ran past the doorway toward the west side of the house.

"Ohhh sweet Lord," exclaimed Gabby. "Bear's out there!"

"Their fighting!" screamed Susan as she bounded into the hallway.

"You can't go out there!" shouted Ray as he grabbed his daughter.

The sound of the confrontation in the back yard was defining as the Mastiff tore into the wolf. Almost immediately, the high-pitched whines of the Mastiff indicated the terrible outcome.

"He's killing Bear!" screamed Susan, as her feet moved desperately, but couldn't find the floor.

"Out of the way!" shouted Gabby.

Muscling past the two in the hallway, the old fellow burst through the screen door, barrel first. Then, as he swung the Bellmore around to the left, he paused as if shocked.

"You sorry, no good--"

The rest of Gabby's comment was cut short by the report of the Bellmore's right barrel. After a very quick pause accented with a confounded gaze, he touched off the left barrel in the same direction.

"More shells!" exclaimed Gabby. He ran back inside, slamming the back door behind him.

Ray, still holding onto his daughter, moved against the wall as Gabby ran toward them. Then, noting Margaret rattling the Super-X box as she stepped quickly from her bedroom, the old fellow smiled for the first time since he woke up.

Sensing the fight had gone badly with Bear, Susan

stopped struggling and went almost limp. "Noooo. Please no," she moaned softly as her tears streaked down her cheeks and quickly found the floor.

"Did you hit him?" asked Margaret as Gabby shoved his hand into the shell box.

Fumbling with the shells and the gun at the same time, Gabby glanced up at Margaret and then looked back at Susan. "He's gone, sweetie," he added as he slowly shook his head. "The first shot was for Bear, 'Pumpkin'. His throat was completely gone but he was still struggling." He then looked at Ray and added, "I put the brass bead right on the beast's nose and pulled the trigger to the full choke side. With number threes, it should've killed 'em, Ray. Did knock 'em down though, but he rolled to his feet and trotted off around the side of the house. Never seen anything quite like it." Gabby broke the shotgun down, flipped out the spent casings, and then slid in two more. "Should've killed him sure," he said again as he shoved a handful of shells into his right, pants pocket. "What about the boy? Have you seen him?" he asked.

Margaret's mouth flew open. Then, as she quickly shook her head, she answered, "With things happening so fast around here, I didn't even think about--"

"I heard him," interrupted Susan as she looked toward the back door. "He ran that way. Something scared him right out of the house."

No sooner had she said that, than someone screamed in the front yard, and it was close, very close.

"That's him," said Margaret. "He's on the front porch," she added as she wheeled and then ran toward the dinning room.

"Get him quick!" exclaimed Susan. She wrenched free of her father and ran to help her mother.

"Don't open that door!" shouted Gabby as he snapped the breech of the Bellmore closed and ran after them.

"Margaret!" shouted Ray. As he quickly followed, he added, "Look, before you open that door!"

Perhaps, she didn't hear him, or maybe it was the sound of Charlie crying on the far side of the door that clouded her judgment. At any rate, just as soon as she got her hand on the knob, she tripped the latch and opened the door.

Crouched down, with his back against the side of the door, the boy rolled backwards against her legs.

"Ohhh, Ray," she managed weakly, staring at the huge wolf, not more than two steps or so from her.

Standing on the steps, with his forepaws on the front porch, the beast remained perfectly still. He looked down at the lad, and then back up to Margaret with the very expression Lassie uses when she looks at Timmy. Then, prompted by the two, metallic clicks of the Bellmore's hammers, it wheeled and trotted off toward the road and the darkness of Black Bottoms.

"Out of the way!" shouted Gabby as he brushed past the group all but blocking the doorway. "Just one more chance, you black devil," he hissed through clinched teeth as he raised the shotgun toward the slowly retreating animal.

"Don't," said Ray. He placed his hand upon the Bellmore. "It could've had you at the back door. It could've taken any of us when Margaret opened this one, and it could've had this boy anytime it wanted from the start."

"Come, child," said Margaret, helping the boy to his feet. "I don't understand any of this, but it looks like you need some more clothes and another bath.

"I'll get another shirt," added Susan. Wiping her tears on her pajama sleeves, she managed, "Dad's only got three more left."

Gabby backed slowly from the porch, pushing the others inside as he went. After closing and locking the door, he looked back through the window. There was no sign at all of morning. The only glow was from the fireplace, casting its golden hue upon everything in the den. Pausing at the doorway, he listened to Margaret trying to calm the boy down. Even though he couldn't help feeling sorry for him, there was just something unusual about him being inside.

"Keep it close," suggested Ray as he nodded toward the Bellmore. "It's barely 2:00am and if we can, we need to try to get some sleep. I'll check the back door again."

"Good grief", mumbled Gabby. He then walked to the end of the couch, leaned the Bellmore against the wall, and then added, "I'm gonna conk out tomorrow if I get woke up again."

* * *

The old riverboat man never heard Margaret put Charlie back on the couch. He barely noted how good the goose-down pillow felt or the pleasant scent of the fresh sheets before he fell asleep once more. But early that morning, barely three hours later, something disturbed him again.

Laying there, half in and half out of sleep, he finally figured out what it was. It was an odor, and a strange one at that. Having been a hunter ever since he was able to cock a 410-gauge shotgun, he knew what a wet dog smelled like. Then, he remembered that Susan said something scared the lad from the house. Susan's playful, werewolf quip, coupled with the smell, suddenly and completely erased the drowsiness from him. Trying not to move at all, he slowly opened his eyes and looked about the room--from the fireplace across from the coffee table, to the recliner on the far side, and then to what he could see of the dining area. Still smelling the pungent odor, he slowly raised his head a bit and looked toward the television and the boy's couch.

He's sitting up, he thought as he batted his eyes to clear the sleep from them.

Then, as things began to take shape, he realized the silhouette was not that of a boy with a quilt over his shoulders, but one that had the pointed ears of a . . .

"All hands on deck! All hands on deck!" shouted Gabby as he rolled off the couch once more.

Scrambling toward the shotgun, he expected to feel the beast's fangs upon his neck at any minute. Then, as he grabbed the Bellmore and swung it over the arm of the couch, the dinning room light came on. Now, with the view of the far couch over the brass bead of the twelve gauge, he could hardly believe his eyes.

"Put down that thing, Gabby!" exclaimed Ray as he briskly entered the room. "What in blazes has got you going this time?"

Gabby slowly lowered the Bellmore and stared wordlessly at the quilt completely covering the boy still sitting up on the couch.

"Check 'em," finally managed the old fellow.

Ray went straight to the couch, slowly uncovered the boy, and then looked at Gabby and said, "He's just fine."

"Exactly," added the old riverboat man as he leaned the shotgun back against the wall.

"Were you about ready to shoot him? Did you have a nightmare?" asked Ray.

Charlie eased from the quilt, silently looking at Gabby.

"Not sure," admitted Gabby, glancing at Susan and Margaret, who were now standing by the dining room doorway. "Somethin's just not right here, Ray," added Gabby. "I know what I saw and it wasn't a dream."

Ray, feeling of Charlie's back, turned to the girls and said, "He's gonna need another shirt. This one is very damp, almost wet."

"Wet?" echoed Margaret. She walked over, felt of his forehead, and then said, "You've got no fever, sweetie, but you certainly need another shirt. Perhaps the fire is a bit too warm."

Charlie said nothing, but kept an eye on Gabby, even when Margaret got in between them.

"This room's not a bit hot," grumbled Gabby. "How do you explain that shirt?"

"Here's another shirt," stated Susan as she quickly walked back into the room. "There's only two left now."

"Not sure how to explain it," admitted Margaret as she helped the boy change.

Finding it difficult for the boy to keep the old riverboat man in sight as Margaret fidgeted with the shirt made Gabby smile a bit. "I see you, young fella," he poked, "And you know what I saw too."

Charlie glared silently at the old man as Gabby eased back to his pillow.

"Bull feathers," grumbled Gabby. "If werewolves were real, I think I'd of seen one by now as old as I am. Got a whole three days off and somethin' weird like this has to happen."

"Gabby?" Margaret edged closer to the bigger couch. "Are you all right?"

The old fellow pushed his blanket back and slowly sat up. "You got a good look at that animal--eyeball to eyeball. It could've had you or the boy. But instead, it turned and left here as calm as a yard dog."

"It did that," replied Margaret.

Ray slowly nodded as he added, "The beast is here because we have the boy," he complained. Gabby then looked at Ray. "I tell you, it-knows-that-boy."

"You draw a good picture, old friend," responded Ray, "But I don't have any answers. Maybe come mornin', we'll find a few more pieces to this puzzle."

Gabby then looked at the Indian. "You know where those pieces are, don't you boy?"

Youngblood slowly collected his pillow and moved to the far arm of the couch. Pulling the sheet and blanket to his chin, he lay silently there, staring at the old riverboat man.

"Fitting," quipped Gabby, nodding at the boy's blanket. It was woven in the colors of night, showing a wolf with a full moon in the background.

Susan, finally showing a bit of a smile, quipped, "You've been watching entirely too many horror movies by yourself."

"Uhhh," grumbled Gabby as he retreated back to his pillow, covering his head with his blanket.

"Enough. 'Uncle' already," quipped Ray. "It's after 5:00am for cryin' out loud. I don't hear a peep out of any of the coon hounds. Everybody back to bed."

"I'm out of here," decided Susan. "Any more of that werewolf stuff and I'll be awake until morning."

* * *

Listening to Gabby's occasional snoring did little to comfort Charlie Youngblood along with the strange smells in the house. The fire was the only thing that now came close to comforting him. Then, the cold riggers came again to the young Indian. Gripping his blanket, he pushed himself back into his goose down pillow and awaited the inevitable. He could now hear every little sizzle and pop of the embers, the scratching sound the little cricket made as it crossed the stone hearth, and the gentle breeze through the pines on the east side of the house. As he watched the embers get notably brighter, the pleasant scent of Margaret's rose soap puzzled him even more; it was in the bathroom. Now, the sweating was starting all over again, and with it, the hot flashes that he knew would soon come to torment him. As he lay there, he caught the scent of something else. It was on the back porch and it wasn't a dog.

"Nooo," he exclaimed, trying to be as quiet as his fear would allow.

Pulling the cover close to his neck, he stuffed the blanket into his mouth and awaited the pain that was soon to come. As his back begin to itch and burn, he tried desperately to rub the cramps from his legs and arms. Then, with watery eyes, he watched in horror as the fireplace began to brighten the entire room. Sobbing quietly beneath his blanket, he quickly recoiled as something touched his shoulder.

"Are you all right, young fella?" asked Gabby as he pulled back the blanket a bit.

"It's coming!" shouted the boy as he snatched the blanket back and then pulled it over his head.

Gabby jumped back, holding his scratched, right hand.

"Here we go again," said Margaret as she and Ray walked back up the hall and turned on the dining room light.

"Never seen anythin' like it," said Gabby, just above a whisper. He's got not a hint of a fingernail, but just look at this."

The old fellow held out his hand to show three, bleeding scratches on the back of his right hand from his wrist to his knuckles.

As Gabby wrapped his bandanna around his hand, Margaret quickly stepped around him and reached for the blanket.

"Step away from the boy," spoke someone from the dining room. The voice was deep, and clearly unfamiliar.

Margaret quickly stepped back and looked toward where the others were already staring. "Ohhh, sweet

Jesus, she said just above a whisper as she looked at the tall Shoshone. He was holding Susan directly in front of him.

His black hair spilled over his shoulders as the soft glow of the fireplace danced in his dark brown eyes as well as the Bowie knife under Susan's chin.

"Don't hurt her. Please, don't hurt her," pleaded Margaret as Gabby backed toward the shotgun.

"Stand still, Old Gray," warned the Indian. "Don't complicate your life more than it has been already."

Gabby froze, noting the hunting knife was closer to Susan's throat.

The Indian then looked at Ray. "Your daughter?" he asked, tapping her chest with the knife.

Ray nodded.

"My son," he then replied with a nod toward the lump in the blanket. "Wise men make deals at times like this—truce even. My son is just now discovering who he really is. His fear of the animal is to be expected. I was simply watching him deal with it."

"Agreed," replied Ray. "What are your terms?"

"My son for your daughter, and . . ." The Indian paused to look at Gabby. "no scattergun, Old Gray."

"Agreed," replied Ray, not waiting for Gabby's answer."

Not saying a word, the Indian continued to stare at Gabby.

"Agreed," Gabby finally echoed, noting the wound on the Indian's left shoulder had already scabbed over.

The Indian returned his knife to its sheath and nodded to his left. "Move away from the boy to the talking box," he instructed, still holding tightly to Susan's arm.

As they moved closer to the television, the Indian gently pushed Susan in their direction and then walked briskly to the couch where Charlie sat, still covered with the blanket. "We go," he said.

He quickly picked up the boy and walked toward the door. Then, pausing there, he slowly looked back and added, "Thank you for your kindness, but do not follow."

His request was accented by a cold stare in Gabby's direction.

"We won't," answered the old riverboat man as the others slowly shook their heads in agreement.

"Wait," exclaimed Susan as the Indian turned to leave. "There's an animal out there that--"

"Susan," interrupted Gabby, grabbing the girl's shoulders.

"But the boy doesn't feel well either," argued Susan.

"That will pass," explained the Indian. "The wolf will not harm the boy, nor will he ever harm you or yours. You've earned this for the kindness you have shown my son." He then looked straight at Gabby. "Gray One," he added sullenly. "A new world is now coming to you. Do not fight it."

The Indian turned and left the house. Rushing to the door, Susan and the others watched as he walked toward the road and Black Bottoms on the far side.

"What's he doing?" asked Susan.

Barely inside the woods, as they looked on, the Indian seemed to be struggling with the boy in the blanket.

"Ohhh my word," said Susan weakly, as something jumped from the Indian's arms and out of the blanket. Rusty brown, with a black saddle across its back and haunches, the cub trotted away from the Indian, looking back occasionally.

"What did I just see?" asked Ray; his eyes were still glued to the window.

"Not sure," answered Gabby. Looking down at the bandanna he was holding on the back of his right hand, he added, "I don't even wan'na guess anymore."

* * *

Back on the front porch of the old Laxton place with his granddaughter, Ray remained strangely quiet as he stared out across the road into Black Bottoms.

"Come," suggested Susan as she took Shelley by the hand. "Let's give Gramps a little break. That was a long story and I think it took a little out of him."

"But what of Gabby?" Shelley looked back at her grandfather and asked again, "What of your friend?"

Ray, smiling slightly, looked at his granddaughter, and then replied, "Our very next trip on the river took us to Baton Rouge. Gabby had family there in a place called

Bluebonnet Swamp. He went to live with them." Slowly looking back toward Black Bottoms, he continued. "Sometimes, when I'm by myself in the woods, I think I hear him, but I guess that's just my wishful thinking." Ray looked back at his granddaughter and added, "Some time ago, he sent me his glasses--the big, thick, horned-rimmed ones. Said he didn't need them anymore and he was doing well and feeling even better. He added that the woods are even more beautiful at night." He smiled at Shelley as he added, "Never saw the boy, the Indian, the wolf, or Gabby ever again. I just hope wolves do well in the swamps of Southern Louisiana."

Second Offering
The Ghost of Queen Anne's Revenge

Around and around there came the sound
of sails popping in the wind.
The Queen Anne she swayed, on her right side she laid,
and swung around us again.
The reaction of those, who stood without prose
could be read on each and every brow.
For Teach they knew well, so as far as they could tell,
not one could save them now. . .

In the wee hours of the morning, Lester Magness lay in his motel room fast asleep. Outside, Beaufort was just waking up. The North Carolina city had just recently gained national notoriety because of a discovery within its coastal waters. It had lain dormant for over two hundred and fifty years on the bottom of Beaufort Inlet. Now, divers based in Fort Fisher were planning to bring up artifacts from the most famous pirate ship that ever sailed salty waters—The Queen Anne's Revenge. Lester, getting word of the North Carolina Underwater Archaeological endeavor, had planned to be there when the first artifact from the Queen Anne's was brought up. Now, all but comatose in his warm, hotel bed in Beaufort, the young writer for Life Magazine was disturbed by an echoing, ships bell.

Much too early to get up, he guessed.

Lester rolled toward the window, but the bright lights of the hotel walkway were no help at all in judging what time it was. Rolling back toward the center of the room, the echoing sound came again—this time it seemed much closer. Pushing up to his right elbow, he looked at the radio clock on the night stand. It glowed 4:00 A M.

Got to have more than six hours.

Flopping back to his pillow, he pulled the covers over his head.

"Come, laddie. Mornin's waistin'."

The strange voice sounded as if it was spoken right into his left ear.

"What!" Lester swung his left hand out toward the intruder, but felt not a thing. Quickly freeing himself of the cover he sat up. But he didn't see anything at all.

Back on his elbow, he looked about the room. Everything was as quiet as a grave, and just about as dark. Lester reached behind him and tugged at the curtains. Now, a bit brighter, he looked about the room again, but saw not a thing. He was just about to lay back down when his eyes focused on the far corner of the room. The heavy, padded chair that was there when he went to bed was gone, or at least it was so dark in that part of the room he couldn't see it.

"That's right, laddie. You're not imaginin' things," the voice spoke again. It was a bit gruff, and the tone of it sounded as if it came from one not used to being ignored.

Like a child, Lester snatched the covers to his chest and tried to look into the darkness where the chair should be. "Who are you?" he managed weakly.

"Let me ship be, laddie. You tell 'em ta let me ship be."

"Who are you?" shouted Lester, hoping someone outside, or at least next door, would hear him.

"All in good time, laddie. I'll be sendin' my man, Caesar to fetch you. Meanwhile, you go and tell 'em to let me ship be or I'll throw 'em to the fishies."

"Throw who?" asked Lester, equally as loud.

A low, maniacal laughter and the scent of nutmeg was as discomforting as the vision now presenting itself in the corner of the room. A face at first, but it was all but hidden by a four-part, platted black beard. Floating in the darkness with a brown, wide-eyed stare, it looked both stern, yet curiously interested. As the apparation turned from him, a vision of an old, sailing vessel lightened that corner of the room. Lester could hear the hardwood heels of his boots pound the wooden wharf as what looked to be a pirate walked away. Dressed in a long, heavy-looking brown coat, his baggy, brown pants were stuffed into the tops of his calf-high, black boots. Lester leaned a bit forward, not only noticing his three-cornered hat, but also the huge sword which was swung low just below his left hip. The vision of both man and ship then faded, leaving the padded chair still sitting in the corner.

With a deep breath, Lester all but tackled the lamp on the nightstand and finally found the on button. Quickly checking the bathroom and closet, he found himself, once again, all alone.

"Can't go back to sleep now," he grumbled. Glancing back at the corner in question, he sat back down on the foot of the bed and pondered, *If I put this in the story, the editor will surely toss it, and then me to boot.* "The Grid Iron is just one block down Orange Street," he decided out loud.

Lester jumped to his feet and walked briskly to the shower. He knew his five-foot-eight, one hundred and sixty-five pound frame was healthy enough, but it was completely dwarfed by the six-foot, ten-inch, two hundred and fifty pound vision he had just seen. Jerking back the shower curtains, he couldn't help but cringe, but there was no one there. Knowing the North Carolina Archeology Group was going to be on the wharf early, he quickly showered and all but ran past the towel. He knew the faster he broke the story of the raising of Queen Anne's Revenge, the more likely the Times editor would take it. With Black Beard's colorful background, and the underwater pictures of the Anne they had already posted, the story would almost write itself.

Stumbling through the living quarters, he quickly dressed, grabbed a light jacket, thumbed his satchel to his shoulder, and then bounded from his room. The wharf was just one block south on Orange Street. One right turn and three blocks later would put him at the Underwater Recovery team's temporary headquarters. Jack Fisher, their publicity man, knew he would be there.

All but jogging from the hotel, Lester looked at his watch. "Almost 5:30 A. M." he said as he pushed on.

Even before he got to the end of Orange Street, he could see the fog had not yet lifted. As he turned west, he noted the glowing, Grid Iron sign in the distance. It's eerie light through fog looked like something out of a 'Strange Encounters' story. Hearing the metallic rattle of equipment and people talking, Lester slowed and looked past the Grid Iron to the end of the wharf, still some seventy-five yards away.

With the aroma of frying beef and potatoes in the air from

the Grid Iron, he pushed on.

Guess breakfast can wait, he thought upon seeing a flashing, blue glow in the fog quite near the Beaufort Expedition trailer.

"Patrol boat," he said as he neared the trailer.

Spotting four, young men walking from the group, Lester slowed as they neared.

"Divers?" he asked.

They nodded, but didn't slow down or speak at all.

"I'm a reporter," lied Lester, now walking with them. "I'm supposed to meet Mr. Fisher at the trailer. What's going on up there?"

One, a tall, lanky, blond fellow replied, "We just came off the Queen Anne. Still haven't found them. We've just been relieved by a Beaufort Search and Rescue team."

"Who's lost?" asked Lester, desperately trying to slow them down.

"Our whole, first diving team—four of them," replied a black-haired fellow. Looking a bit more troubled than the rest, he added, "My brother, Robert Carpenter, is on that team and they ran out of air three hours ago."

"Excuse us," interrupted the blond-haired fellow. "We've got to eat and be back to relieve them in two hours or so."

"Sure." Turning back toward the trailer, Lester pulled his Nikon from his satchel and snapped some spooky, dream-like pictures as he approached another group.

As he drew nearer, a patrol officer noticed him and positioned himself right in his path. "Are you with the

Search and Rescue bunch or the Beaufort Expedition Team?" he asked politely.

"Neither. I'm here to meet with Mr. Jack Fisher. I have some information about those who are lost. Can you take me to the one in charge of the Beaufort Team?"

"Wait right here," responded the officer.

Lester watched him step back a bit to make a call on his shoulder-mounted radio to someone named John Winston. In less than a minute, the officer was escorting him toward the trailer where three men stood watching them from the porch.

As they neared, a tall, stout-looking fellow in his forties stepped from the porch to meet them. "I'm John Winston," he said with an extended hand. Lester's hand all but disappeared in the big fellow's grip.

"I'm Lester Magness. I'm on assignment from Life Magazine. I hurried here as fast as I could after getting word from a Mr. Jack Fisher. Now it seems that I'm in the middle of yet another story."

"Just a minute." John turned toward the porch. "Come here, Jack. This young fellow's a writer for Life." Looking back at Lester, he added, "Jack Fisher is our public relations man, but he can help you later. Right now I want you to tell me what you know about our lost team."

Lester paused, musing just how to go about this without being deemed an insensitive prankster.

"This is going to sound a bit strange, Mr. Winston, but just bear with me and give me the benefit of a doubt."

"Fair enough." Mr. Winston crossed his arms and looked down at him over his glasses.

"First of all," started Lester, "I believe your crew is still alive."

Mr. Winston immediately spun around and waved toward the rescue boat. "Hold up a minute. I might have something for you." Looking back at Lester, he added, "Make it quick."

"Well, to start, I don't believe in ghosts. I also didn't know you had lost a crew until early this morning. Word came to me in a way I have never experienced before then."

Mr. Winston took a long, deep breath and then managed, "My patience is wearing a bit thin, young fellow. If this is some sort of a sick joke, you'll find my sense of humor is nonexistent right about now."

"I can understand that," said Lester, "This morning I was disturbed from sleep by what sounded like a ship's bell. When I awoke, this person was standing in the far corner of my room."

"Did he tell you who he was?" The doubtful look over the glasses was there again.

"No, and if I tell you what he looked like, you would think me daft."

John's eyes narrowed. "Is this the ghost part?"

"Yes, but—"

Cursing under his breath, John wheeled around. Waving at the rescue boat, he shouted, "Cast off. We have nothing here."

Knowing the man, Jack stepped between him and Lester. "Wait just a minute, John," he said as he was all but pushed back toward Lester. "Give the kid a chance. I wan'na hear this."

"Fine." The big fellow glared at Lester. "But if he's paddin' his story, I'm goin' through you to kick his butt. Jimmy's with that group."

Looking back at Lester, Jack said, "He's talking about a Mohawk kid named Jimmy Horseman, his adopted son. I'd make this good if I were you."

The police officer stepped a bit closer, eying Lester and John.

"This is God's truth," started Lester, looking directly at John. "The vision I saw was some kind of mariner. He looked like he stepped right off one of those eighteenth century, three masted sailing ships. He said for me to tell them, that being you people, to let his ship be. He also said if you didn't, he would throw them to the fishies. I believe he was referring to your divers, Sir."

John rolled his eyes. "And you want us to believe that old Teach, himself, spoke to you directly to go and warn us?"

Jack looked back at John.

"Don't look at me." John shook his head. "I don't know where else to look for them either."

Shaking his head disappointedly, Jack looked at Lester and said, "You had best leave. I wouldn't add to that story right now if I were you."

"Go on now," echoed the cop, pulling at Lester's arm. "If you come back here, I'll arrest you for hampering the team."

With the early-morning fog still in the inlet, Lester shouldered his satchel and walked back toward the Gridiron. Halfway there he heard a flute-like sound he couldn't recognize. As he slowed, he searched about for the sound coming out of the fog, now quite close to him.

"An ocarina?" he mused, but still could see nothing in the mist. Giving up on seeing anything, he continued. *Just blew my angle on the whole story,* he thought as a bell sounded in the fog causing the sound of the little wind instrument to stop.

"Strange," said Lester just above a whisper.

But before he could continue, a man stood from one of the wharf benches and approached him. "Got a light?" he asked.

"Don't smoke," replied Lester. But the young man stepped closer, pulled his hood over his head, and then eyed his satchel. "Actually, I'm trying to make a five spot," he added.

"Sorry, I don't have any extra . . ." Lester's voice trailed off watching the stranger put his hand into his jacket pocket.

Then, with a quick glance toward the trailer, he produced a small pistol. "What's in the satchel?" he all but whispered.

Drawing the satchel closer to him, Lester replied, "Just an old I-pad, a camera, and a paper tablet. I only have forty bucks on me. Please leave me my I-pad and camera."

Lester quickly pulled out his billfold and handed him the two twenties. The man sniffed, wiped his runny nose on his right shirt sleeve, and then looked back at him. Smiling, he snatched the two bills and then reached for the satchel.

"Please, just take the money," pleaded Lester, tightening his grip on the satchel.

Without another word, the man swung the revolver up and struck the right side of Lester's head. Everything seemed to explode into black with white stars as he stumbled backwards. With the feel of the wharf's rail behind his thighs, he fell but hardly felt hitting the water.

Sputtering and chocking, the freezing wet jolted him back into the conscious world. Frantically swimming toward the shimmering wharf light on the surface, he fought his way back to the top. Coughing and spitting up what he had just swallowed, the movement of two figures on the wharf quickly drew his attention. The first seemed to be two feet off the boards and was being shaken like a rag doll. His assailant, a particularly large fellow, was not as easy to see. Although he was but a shadowy figure, the cut of his hat and clothes gave him away right off."

"Sir," called Lester, "I need your . . ."

"Leave him be, laddie," spoke another man from just behind him.

Before Lester cold turn around, the arm of a black man reached over his right shoulder. "Come aboard, Sir," he said loudly. "Leave the Captain be. He's collectin' your possibles."

In his mid-forties and graying slightly, the black man stood barely five and a half feet tall. He lifted Lester from the water, drug him onto the wooden deck of some large vessel, and then stood over him smiling. Missing his two front teeth, the spaces seemed to highlight the friendless in his eyes. As Lester rubbed the goose-egg sized bump on his right temple, something caught his eye by his right hand—the little wind instrument he had heard previously in the fog.

"Is this yours?" asked Lester, holding it up toward the little fellow.

"And here it is again," he quipped, obviously pleased. "I'm all the time losin' it, but it always finds its way right back to me. Just like the Queen Anne I'd say."

"The what?" managed Lester, just now noticing the movement of the ship.

It was almost as if it were alive. Gently rolling left and then right, it moved him back and forth as if in invisible hands.

"First time on the water, laddie?" asked the black man.

"First time on any boat," replied Lester.

"They call me Caesar. Captain told me to pull you from the soup while he 'talked' to your friend on the wharf. Can you stand?"

"Standing is not a problem," answered Lester now with both hands on the wooden deck. "I've never been on a floor that was moving like this one."

"It's a deck, laddie," corrected Caesar, "and the Anne is a ship. Don't you be callin' it a boat in front of His Nibs."

"Yes, Sir."

With a laugh that seemed to echo off of everything on the ship, Caesar reached down, took Lester by the shoulders, and then raised him to his feet. Lester could now see most of the others who he had heard laughing. Some were sitting on the hatch covers, while others leaned against the hand railings or sat just under the fog that seemed to be captured in the rigging above.

"I am not a 'Sir'," corrected Caesar as he brushed Lester off. "There," he added proudly. "Good as new."

Pulling at his shirt and jacket, Lester could readily see and feel his completely dry clothes. "I was just in the water, Caesar. How is it that I'm dry now? Am I dreaming?"

Hearing the echoing sound of laughter again, Lester slowly looked about him and upwards toward what the fog would allow him see of the rigging. The crew, many more than just a few, were still watching him closely. He felt as if he was about to direct their path in some way.

"Gentleman," exclaimed Caesar, "this fine, young man is Lester Magness." He quickly reached toward Lester and patted him on the right shoulder. "He is the Captain's guest and will be treated as such."

"Aye Caesar," they all replied in unison.

Lester's gaze followed one of the near ropes from its belaying pin below the hand rail. Its destination was still hidden by the fog. "Where am I?" he asked weakly.

Laughter rose again from those watching.

"Why, you're on the Queen Anne's Revenge out of Beaufort Bay. Right now, we're off the coast of the Carolinas. Headin' a bit south-east I would say. His Nibs has struck a kind of deal with Governor Hide. We are allowed to 'escort' the Sugar Ship back to Beaufort for a closer look at her cargo."

The whole crew burst out in another round of laughter.

Nodding toward the elated bunch, Caesar added, "We keep the rum. The Captain and the Governor will deal with the sugar and cocoa at Ocracoke."

"And why am I here?" asked Lester.

Caesar, wheeling around toward the others, shouted, "Mathew!"

"Aye Caesar," responded a tall, dark-haired white fellow.

Stepping from the group gathered at the second hold toward the stern, he studied Lester closely.

"Take him to the Captain's room. His Nibs will be along when he gets there. Tend to his needs."

"Aye Caesar," replied the man, taking hold of Lester's right arm.

"Wait a minute," interrupted Lester. "Can't you just put me back on the wharf? I have a lot of work to—"

The smile on Caesar's face and the laughter from the others quickly answered Lester's question.

"Shhh," hissed Caesar. "The Anne will not be turning back laddie. We will headin' back after we deal with the Sugar Ship. Besides, don't worry 'bout Time here. It seems ta stand still as it were."

"Come," encouraged Mathew. Leading Lester toward the stairway down to the second deck he added, "Best be mindin' what the Captain or Caesar tells you. Teach told Caesar that he needed your help. Something about keeping the Anne afloat." Mathew nodded toward the bow as they stepped down the stairs. "Just remember, there are worse things that could happen. You could find yourself in the hold with his other 'guests'."

Looking toward the bow, past a row of cannons on either side of an aisle, Lester noted another railing. It protected yet another set of stairs leading down to a third deck and possibly the hold to which Mathew had just referred.

"I believe I'll pass on that one," replied Lester weakly.

"Come then," instructed Mathew, turning the lad around.

Walking toward the stern, and between more cannons, Lester could see two, oil lanterns on either side of a heavy, oaken door. As he passed, the gun crews stopped and nodded, but said not a word. The men were dressed in loose-fitting tunics, with baggy pants, and leather shoes that looked more like house slippers. Most sported beards, but those that didn't had faces that looked more weathered than any others he had ever met.

Mathew stopped at the door, glanced at Lester, and then knocked twice. Upon receiving no reply, he opened the door and pushed Lester inside in front of him.

Pointing toward a couch and padded chair, Mathew said, "Have a seat. I'll be getting somethin' for you and the Captain to eat and drink. He's always hungry when he comes back." Looking straight at Lester, he added, "And when he does come, his name is 'Sir' to you and not Captain. Be polite to him and you just might make it out of this 'Devil's Dodge'."

"Yes, Mathew," replied Lester just above a whisper.

After Mathew shut the door, Lester slowly looked about the spacious room. Larger than the average bedroom, it smelled of fresh hewn oak and lacquer. With mounted oil lamps on the walls every five feet or so, he could readily see that there were no windows on either side of the room or on the wall either side of the door. But, looking past a huge desk toward the stern, he could see a set of beveled windows across the entire back wall. Starting eighteen inches from the floor, they reached all the way to the eight-foot ceiling.

Looking closely at the front of the desk, he read the engraving, "The Concorde, Captain Benjamin Harringold."

To the left of the desk, and secured against the wall, rested a heavy-looking mahogany chest. Of very dark wood, and polished brass stays and hasp, it sported a domed lid, equally well appointed. Lester crept toward it. On a closer look at the hasp, he could see the lock was shut, but the hasp was not behind it. One wooden barrel stood on either side of the chest. They looked to be stuffed with rolled up maps. Back to the chest, Lester's imagination ran wild as he eyed the hasp. But looking atop the chest, he spotted two, Hammer Hill, forty caliber pistols with walnut grips and golden hammers. Picking one up, he looked at it closely. He had just about drummed up the nerve to peep inside the chest when someone spoke from behind him.

"Think hard on that, Laddie," said the man.

Spinning around, Lester glanced toward the closed door and then to the desk. The same man in his dream was now sitting behind it, smiling at him.

Looking a bit amused, he quipped, "Ya gonna shoot me, laddie?"

"I . . . I didn't hear you come in, Sir," managed Lester, quickly laying the pistol back beside its mate.

"Not many do." Pointing at a straight chair close to the left side of the window, he added, "Pull up a chair. I'll be havin' a word or two with you."

"Yes, Sir," replied Lester.

Turning toward the chair, he could see a coat rack. A heavy, brown coat rested upon it, with a three-cornered hat at its top. Completely damp and dripping puddles on the floor, he also noted his satchel. It was resting in the very chair he was about to move.

"Thanks for that," said Lester, glancing back.

The Captain nodded.

After pulling the chair to the front side of the desk, he sat down and added, "Sir, I don't understand any of this."

Teach smiled, leaned back in his padded chair, and then just looked at him. For the first time, Lester could plainly see his face. The scar across the bridge of his nose, and down the left side of his cheek looked as if they had healed without stitches. His black beard, at least a foot long, consisted of four, platted lengths—one on each of his shoulders and the other two resting on his chest. The length of his heavy mustache could not be judged for its ends were hidden within the two, platted lengths upon his chest.

Without another word, the Captain got up and walked to a little, potbellied stove on the port side of the room. After stoking it with wood from a box on its right, he looked back at Lester. "Simple," he answered as he closed the stove's door. "I've done you a favor, and now it's time to return it." Smiling again at Lester, he added, "I was pardoned by the King, you know. Seventeen-eighteen it was. I tried to stay away from her I did, but the call o' tha sea got stronger every day."

"From her?" Lester squinted his eyes.

"The sea, laddie! The sea!" Replied Teach. He nudged the little stove as if testing its moorings on the floor. "The hard ground had no soul. It hurt my feet. Then, that North Carolina Governor Hyde made me an offer. A Spanish tradin' ship out of Jamaica he wanted. Made the run three times a year she did. Carried rum, sugar, cocoa, and sometimes script. I knew it would be as easy as pickin' a plum." He looked up and laughed loudly. Dragging a straight back chair close to the stove, he sat back down, and then added, "That's when it started all over again. After the Sugar Ship, we blocked the whole port of Charleston, South Carolina. They had nothin' there to match the Queen Anne."

"You took Charleston hostage?"

"Weren't no battle, boy. We lay off the harbor until a big cargo ship put out from her. It were thirty two guns to six. We took what we wanted plus a dozen, rich-lookin' citizens to barter with. After we threatened to hang em', the good people of Charleston gave us what we wanted. Sadly, that's when I made my mistake. In my anger at the Governor, I cursed him." He smiled at Lester. "Old Scratch that is," he added softly.

"Old Scratch?" Lester eyed him curiously.

"The Devil, you pelican! Ain't you ever heard of Satan?"

Lester nodded.

"Well, he now controls this place." Teach pointed to the floor of the room. "After I took Charleston, I believe he sent one o' his angels to talk to that Governor Alexander Spotswood. Never did like Virginia anyways. Spotswood by himself was next to nothin', but he had the English navy right there with him at the time. He sent Commander Maynard to do his biddin'. Chased me through a shallow inlet at Beaufort he did. Beached the Anne right there on a sand bar I did, tryin' to get her port guns into play."

Lester slowly looked about the room and finally asked, "He sunk the Queen Anne?"

"I sunk it!" shouted Teach, kicking the stove so hard it separated from the floor on its right side, pulled loose from its stovepipe, and then fell to the floor.

Scrambling from the spilling wood, ashes, and embers, Lester noted that Teach had not moved at all. He just smiled, watching him closely.

"Sat back down, Laddie," he said softly. "Watch and see."

Obviously, Lester knew that an object such as a stove couldn't move on its own. But as he watched, the live coals started moving first. Following them, the ashes and the wood slid right back into the stove. Then, with a click of its door, the little stove righted itself upon the floor and reconnected with the above stovepipe as well as the floor beneath it.

"What the Devil . . ." said Lester weakly as he watched the nails reseat themselves in its cat-like feet.

Slapping his knee soundly, Teach laughed out loud at Lester's expression. "What do ya see about you, Laddie?" he added loudly, pointing to the stove, the unmarred floor, and the walls about them. "Don't ya see? The Queen Anne lives because of 'em. She dies every year and us along with her. Afresh the next spring at the first robin's call, we rise and pull her off that dammed bar at Beaufort's Inlet. Chasin' the first fog that presents itself, we head for the coast of the Carolinas again. But now, He's takin' us where I don't need to go!" Looking at Lester, he added, "They've found her, Laddie! They've found the Anne and now they're pullin' her very soul apart, piece by piece!" Slowly looking solemnly at Lester, he added softly. "When they raise her bell from the water . . ."

Teach's voice trailed off as he looked at the fire through the slits in the stove's door. For the first time, Lester saw a hint of fear in his face.

"What happens when they bring the bell up, Sir?" asked Lester.

"Old Scratch comes for his own," he answered weakly. Looking back at Lester, he added, "When we get back to Beaufort, I'll be callin' on you to carry a message to who-ever captains those diving people I have in the hold. If they expect to ever see their crew again, they'll quit pickin' at my ship."

Teach stopped talking and looked toward the door.

"Hear something, Sir?" Lester looked toward the door also.

"Not a sound, Laddie. Waitin' for Gibbs—Garrat Gibbens that is. He's my Boatswain."

"Boatswain?"

"Deck foreman, sort of."

Just as soon as Teach explained the meaning, two loud knocks came upon the door.

Smiling at Lester, Teach said loudly, "Come!"

As the door opened, Lester could readily see a stout-looking, blond-haired young fellow step halfway inside. At six feet, four inches tall, he was almost Teach's size but fifteen years or more his junior.

"The fog's lifting, Sir." He looked at Lester, almost studying him.

"And the 'Plum'?" asked Teach.

"She's ten miles this side of Jamaica this time, Captain, and three miles off our port bow."

"Plum?" asked Lester.

Giving the lad an irritable glance, Teach snapped, "The Sugar Ship, ya pelican. Ain't ya been payin' attention?"

Smiling at the bit of green showing in the lad, Gibbs looked back at the Captain and added, "The gun crews are at the cannons, Sir. Others with hooks and pike poles are hidden. We're showing a dozen crew and officers in English red and the 'Fightin' Jack' is flying on the main."

"Good." Teach stood, pushing his chair away from the stove. "You're a wizard at lies, Mr. Gibbens. Send John Carnes into the riggin' with two long rifles. At the signal, tell him to take out the helmsman."

"Aye Captain. Is that all?"

"That's enough, Mr. Gibbs. We'll be along directly."

Teach walked around the stove, grabbed a windbreaker from the rack on the wall, and pitched it to Lester. Without a word, he put on his heavy coat, threw his sword belt over his right shoulder, and then donned his three-cornered hat.

"Come, Laddie," he said, glancing back at Lester, "This'll be somethin' ta tell your grandchildren about."

Following Teach closely, the young writer walked right out the door, down between at least sixteen cannons, and then paused at the top of a fifteen foot opening in the main deck.

"Just off our port bow about a mile, sir," shouted John Carnes from the crow's nest.

The trim, dark-haired young man was leaning precariously from a mast-mounted, four foot basket looking through a spyglass at a set of brilliant, white sails in the distance.

"How's she dressed, Mr. Carnes?" asked Teach.

"Two masts, bearing main sails and jibs, Captain. Four cannon I can see—four pounders probably. She's coming quickly, Sir, but not as fast as she's able."

Picking his steps carefully, Lester eased from the Captain's side and to the hand railing along the wall as the Ann pushed through yet another six-foot wave.

"Mr. Gibbs," said Teach loudly.

"Aye, Sir," responded the boatswain, stepping a bit closer to the main deck railing to look at the Captain. He had donned a red, English officer's coat.

"Put Stephen Daniels, Tom Gates, and Joe Gills on the bow with their rifles."

"Aye, Sir." Gibbs quickly disappeared from the railing.

"Come here, Laddie," said Teach. Grabbing the young writer by the right shoulder, the Captain pushed him a bit away from the hole to the second deck. "Get up there in front of the wheel. You can't see nothin' down here. Stand right there in front of the helmsman with Lieutenant Richards. I'll be up directly."

"Yes, Sir." Lester eyed the steps cautiously.

"Mr. Husk," called Teach as he pushed Lester toward the steps to the wheel.

"Aye, Captain," answered a trim, brown-haired fellow standing between the cannons toward the bow.

"Keep them hull doors closed on your cannons 'till we strike the 'Jack'."

"Aye, Sir," came the reply.

Holding tightly to the handrail, Lester climbed the steps to the wheel. The salt spray in the air wisped over the Anne at every five seconds. Lester counted them out as he eased up beside Lieutenant Richards. The English-looking fellow was about his size, all of forty years old, and had blond hair protruding from the rear of his three-cornered hat. The officer pulled on his pipe, nodded politely, and then looked toward the approaching ship.

"Where is the forward hold, Sir?" asked Lester.

The Lieutenant gestured with his pipe back toward the second deck. "There's a set of stairs at the end of the cannon isle. It leads to the hold."

"The French ship nears, Captain," said the Lieutenant.

Teach glanced up and then ordered, "Come about well off her bow, Mr. Richards. Don't excite them toward a closer look. I don't want to have to chase down and perhaps damage the sloop to catch her. We have to sail her back to Beaufort after all."

"Very well, Sir." The Lieutenant then looked to the helmsman and ordered, "Come about on my orders."

"Aye, sir."

Then, just as they passed the sleek, white, two-master, Lieutenant Richards gave the order with but the point of his right, index finger. The helmsman spun the Anne's wheel as quickly as he could to port. Laying sharply on her starboard side, the quick maneuver sent

Lester to his knees and grappling for a tighter hold on the railing.

Formerly the 'Concorde', the sleek, three-masted Queen Anne's Revenge danced around the sloop in not much more than fifteen seconds.

Teach stepped from the second deck, stood Lester back to his feet, and then stepped to the port side of the ship in plain sight. Caesar, running up the stairway, ran to him. Gripping two pistols, handles first, he held them out to Teach.

The Captain quickly took the weapons and stuck them behind his belt. "Come, Mr. Richard's," he added loudly, "let us test the metal of Mr. Hyde's Sugar Ship once more."

"Very well, Sir," answered the Lieutenant.

With a single point toward the crow's nest from Lieutenant Richards, the rifleman therein, cocked his weapon, waited until they were about even with the smaller ship, and then fired.

With gray smoke rolling through the Anne's sails, Lester quickly looked toward the Sugar Ship's quarter deck. He could see their helmsman slumping over the far side of the big wheel. As it slowly laid him upon the deck, the sloop gently swayed to port.

"You killed him!" said Lester loudly.

Gibbs, quickly stepping to Lester's side, said, "Have you lost your mind, boy. Give a mind to where you are."

"Strike the Jack, Mr. Gibbs," exclaimed the Lieutenant. "Run up the 'Jolly Roger'. Let them know who we really are." He looked back at the helmsman. "Come about and catch her," he shouted.

The helmsman quickly spun the wheel to the port again laying the Queen heavily on her starboard side sending Lester grabbing for the railing again.

"Mr. Husk," shouted Teach to the gunnery officer on the second deck.

"Aye, Sir," came the answer.

"Bring your port guns to bear. Let 'em see what a real cannon looks like afore they get foolish with those pop guns."

"Aye, Sir."

Sounding a bit like thunder, sixteen heavy hull doors were dropped open against the side of the Queen Anne. Lester quickly looked below to the gunnery deck. Each crew on the port side was wrestling with the mooring ropes, slowly inching the two-thousand pound cannons forward.

Now, with sixteen black muzzles bristling from the Queen Anne's port side, the captain of the Sugar Ship slowly removed his hat at the horrifying spectacle. The crew of the Anne, in plain sight now, were dancing, twirling grappling ropes, and taunting those on the Sugar Ship.

The sloop's crew, however, could only stand there and watch Fate take over.

"Lieutenant Richards," said Teach.

"Aye, Sir."

"Trim to ten yards if you will, Sir."

"She's not slowing, sir," complained the helmsman.

"Mr. Husk," shouted Teach.

"Aye, Sir."

"Put a chain into her jibs, but harm not the bow."

Firmly uncomfortable with the command, the gunnery officer pushed the gunner away from the first cannon. Carefully sighting it himself, he set fire to the powder.

Lester barely had time to notice two hands running from the sloop's bow before the defining roar came. Thick gray smoke billowed across the water toward the hapless vessel. Quickly looking back toward the sloop's bow, he could see splinters of the poles and fragments of the sails flying away from just above the smaller ship's bow. Almost instantly, their mainsail was struck, as was the Anne's. Now, within fifteen yards, a dozen grappling hooks streaked their beige-colored ropes toward the sloop while as many pike pokes stood at the ready to maintain a safe distance.

"Set up the boarding plank," shouted Gibbs.

Noting that all eyes were now on the captured ship, Lester remembered what the Lieutenant said and backed away from the helm. Easing down the steps toward the gunnery deck, he looked toward the bow and into its shadows. With all hands still more concerned with the Sugar Ship, he walked briskly down the gunnery isle toward the bow.

There it is, he thought as the guard rail came into view.

Still not gaining the attention of anyone, and with the diving crew heavily on his mind, he quickly eased down the steps a bit and peeped into a much darker place. With only two, oil lamps burning on the wall to his left, the hold was very dim at best. Then, as his eyes focused on some wooden barrels toward the stern, someone spoke to him to his left.

"Over here," spoke the person. So close it was it made him jump.

An arm was sticking out from a small window in a door in the wall. The waterproof watch on its wrist was all Lester needed to know. He had found the divers.

#

Back on the Sugar Ship, Teach stood aside the boarding plank while his crew collected weapons and valuables from the crew and hold. Not allowing anyone to approach the Sugar Ship's quarter deck, he stood there eying the captain. The wiry-looking Frenchman, well into his fifties, glared angrily back at him. His hand slowly rose to where a pistol handle protruded from his belt.

"Now, Sir," quipped Teach. "I have a dozen rifleman and sixteen two-thousand pounders pointed right at you. Don't bite off mor'n you're able to chew."

The smile on Teach's face usually backed up most men, but the Frenchman stood his ground. "Black-bearded devil," he mumbled. "What will you do with us?" he asked a bit louder.

"My carpenter, Mr. Roberts, is having a look at your bow. If it's still seaworthy, you will be taken to Beaufort Bay and released. We will, however, keep your ship and everything on it as spoils of war."

Teach had no sooner finished than two rifle shots rang out from the bow of the Anne. Glancing to where they were pointed, Teach quickly looked back up into the sloop's rigging as a long rifle hit the deck a bit in front of him. A young sailor was hanging by his hands from crow's nest. Another rifle spoke from the Anne, releasing his hold on the basket. The body of the young sailor crashed through the door of the forward hold.

"You'll pay for this, Teach!" shouted the captain of the sloop, but he didn't touch his pistol.

"I already am," laughed Teach.

"Captain," called someone from the Anne.

Quickly turning, Teach spotted Gibbs on the far side of the boarding plank. "You had best come and see this, Sir," he finally said. "Words fail me."

Teach walked briskly from the sloop, across the boarding plank, and then stopped in front of Gibbs. "Well? Why must I be called back before I'm finished with the sloop?"

"Look toward the aft section of the gunnery deck, Sir."

The Captain hastily walked to the steps, went halfway down them, and then stopped. The gunnery crews were now gathering under the main deck opening, looking from Teach, to the last six vacant, gun ports, and back again. They remained strangely quiet. Gazing into the dim light of the gunnery deck, he stood
there dumfounded. The last six cannons were not there.

"Here they are," shouted a sailor as he stepped from the forward hold stairs and onto the gunnery deck with the four divers. "We've been jinxed by these! Get shed of these men right now or we'll all be doomed!"

"Joseph Brooks," exclaimed Teach, seeing he was pulling Lester up behind him. "What's happening with the gunnery deck? Where are my cannons?"

Mr. Brooks, a stumpy, hot-headed, second mate, shoved Lester to the deck, but held to the back of his collar. The four divers were then forced from the stairway by five other sailors. As they were pushed to the floor beside Lester, the second mate glared at Teach, but said nothing.

Teach eased his hand close to his forty caliber pistols. Mr. Brooks knew that gesture well. It was the last 'word' in any of his arguments or orders.

Looking at Brooks, Teach said, "It would be in your favor if my second mate didn't place blame here, Mr. Brooks. There's none to blame here but the Devil himself. Now, release the boy."

"I'll not!" shouted Brooks as he pulled his sheath knife.

Before the weapon could be placed to Lester's throat, Teach pulled and fired one of the Hammer Hills. Brook's body jerked. His head lolled back on his shoulders as if he were looking up at the main deck. Slowly, he dropped the knife and sank to his knees. A trickle of red oozed out of the nickel-sized hole in his forehead, across his cheek, and then worked its way down the left side of his chin. In horror, Lester grabbed the man and lowered him to the deck. He then turned, watching the one called Black Beard closely. But before another word could be said, a loud, banging noise came from the main deck.

"We've lost the boarding plank, Sir," said Gibbs, looking down from the main deck. "The Sloop is pulling away from us."

Charging up the stairs, Teach mumbled, "Is everything becoming unglued as I watch?"

"What now Mr. Gi . . ." Teach's voice trailed off as he noted the Sugar Ship. It was silently moving away. Lieutenant Richards was waving and shouting on the main deck back to them, but his voice sounded afar off. Looking a bit like a faded painting, the smaller ship drifted away from the Queen Anne.

"Look, Sir," said Gibbs weakly. Pointing toward the stern of the sloop, he added, "It leaves no wake."

"Captain!" screamed the horrified helmsman.

Even with two steps closer to the quarter deck, Teach could see no trace of the Anne's wheel in front of the man.

The Bell, thought Teach, quickly looking to the right of the helmsman. "There was no trace of the bell! Where tha Devil's home is it!"

"Captain?" spoke someone from behind him. The word was spoken so weakly, he could hardly hear it.

Now, firmly set in a place he had never been before, Black Beard was facing a foe he could not touch. Slowly turning, he looked at his long-time friend and confident, Caesar. They both stood there without a word. The old, black man was looking down at his hands. They, like the rest of his body was slowly becoming transparent.

"Captain?" said Caesar once more, and then he was gone.

Teach spun around in horror, looking toward the Sugar Ship in the distance, to the rigging of the Anne, and then down to the gunnery deck toward Lester and the divers. What was left of the crew were quickly gathering about on the main deck and below the main deck opening. They were all silently looking at him. Without words, they faded into the air like so much ground fog on a cool, spring morning. Then, hearing what sounded like thunder, Teach looked off the port bow toward a massive, on-coming storm. The angry-looking clouds were slowly settling from the heavens to the water and rolling gently toward the Queen Anne.

"Get up here!" ordered Teach, looking down at Lester and the divers.

As they scrambled up the steps to the main deck, the Queen Anne shuddered violently causing them to cling to the hand railing. As if orchestrated by Neptune himself, the great fighting ship's bow gently moved toward the storm now gathering on the port side of the ship.

"Sir?" managed one of the divers as they ran to the Captain's side. "I am Jimmy Horseman—a Mohawk. I think this not to be a curse. But it is a coming of something I do not yet understand. I smell a stench in the air. Something's burning and it is not wood." Jimmy then nodded toward the low, clouds and flashing lightning. "If the ship takes us into that place I believe we will never come out. We have to leave her right now, Sir."

Looking down at the deck, and then back up to Lester, Teach replied, "I hold no grudge to any of you. You are released of any debt to me. But you cannot help me now. Stayin' here is not wise for any of you, but I feel I have little choice."

With that, he pulled his sword and pointed it at

Lester. "Take the divers from my ship, laddie. This is somethin' I must do by myself."

Having said that, Teach placed the tip of his sword on the young writer's chest and backed him toward the port side with the divers. Lester couldn't take his eyes off the man somehow. Even when he counted four splashes, he still stared at the one called Blackbeard.

"Aren't you coming, Sir?" asked Lester. "Surely, you're not staying here."

The dismal countenance of the Captain broke instantly with an uncontrollable laughter. "Laddie . . ." he finally managed, "I ain't been here for two hundred and ninety five years." Still laughing, he leaned toward Lester and shoved something into the young writer's pocket. "Off with you, boy," he shouted, as he shoved him over the hand railing.

Fighting his way back to the surface, Lester turned until he could spot the Queen Anne. Teach was as far up on the bow as he could get.

As the great ship drew near the storm, he held his sword high and shouted, "Come, ya devil! Take me if ya can, Beelzebub! And damn ya . . . if ya do!"

"Do you hear that?" said someone behind Lester.

The young writer spun around to see Jimmy swimming up to join him.

Pushing his log, black hair from his face, Jimmy added, "I can hear the sizzling and snapping of a fire from here. That is not lightning in those black clouds. It's the devil's furnace I think."

"Shhh," hissed Lester as he watched the Queen's stern disappear into the dark clouds. "Come," he added, motioning to the four divers. "Stay as close to me as you can."

Now, holding to each other, the black clouds slowly rolled over them. But, strangely enough, the ocean stopped churning and gradually became as calm as a small lake. Then, with a crash that sounded as if God had slammed a great door, the eerie light faded from the midst of the clouds causing them to change into as much light fog.

"What was that?" asked Jimmy, gripping Lester's arm tightly.

"I'm not even going to guess," replied Lester.

"Be quiet," shouted one of the other divers. "I can hear a ship's bell.

"Please," pleaded Lester. "No more bells."

"We're in Beaufort Inlet," exclaimed another diver. "I can see Carrot Island."

Hearing a motor start close behind them, they all turned to see their diving boat powering toward them.

"That's John Winston on the bow," shouted Jimmy, waving excitedly at the man.

"Robert Carpenter," shouted John. "Is that you and your team I'm lookin' at?"

"And then some, John!" shouted Robert. "We're here with a reporter no less—Lester Magness."

"Where the devil have you been? We've been lookin' for you for almost a solid twenty-four hours."

With everyone in the water laughing, Jimmy finally said, "We'll let Lester do that for us. He makes his living with words. Perhaps he can now find the right ones for us."

"Well . . ." John eyed Lester as he pulled Jimmy into the boat. "I know you," he finally said, grabbing the young man and hoisting him aboard. "You're the practical joker who tried to sell us on that ghost story. How is it that you're with my divers?"

Running his hand into the pocket of the old windbreaker he still had on, Lester pulled out a golden coin. Handing it up to John, he added, "You can keep that. I'll keep this old raincoat. They were both given to me by the one you call Blackbeard.

Through the cheers and applause of all those on the diving boat, Lester tried as best he could to explain things. But the only sound that could be heard over everyone else, was John Winston, rebuffing the young reporter as he related their Queen Anne's Revenge experience.

Third Offering:
Bright Rider

Ashley Nutt and her sister Hailey relaxed calmly in a small pond situated under a little waterfall near the rear of their home. The sound of the bubbling water from their spring as it cascaded off a huge stone above the teenagers proved completely relaxing. With her hazel eyes shut, the eighteen-year-old Ashley completely missed the reed tops moving at the far end of their swimming hole. Her younger sister, however, didn't miss the subtle movements at all. The little pool, thirty feet at its widest part, was only fifty feet long and four feet at its deepest point. Ashley lay at its south end with her head resting on one of the many flat stones that bordered the pond. Hailey brushed her black hair from her face and eyed the wiggling reeds on the north side. Now, plainly uncomfortable, she worked her way out of the deeper part and closer to her sister.

"Ashley," she whispered, but her older sister moved not a muscle. "Ashley," she whispered again, adding a bit of a nudge.

"What?" Responded the pretty redhead as she slowly sat up and washed the sleep from her eyes. "The evening's almost gone," she complained. "The old Mississippi is much too dingy to bathe in and this is just too tempting."

"I think your Noah is peeping at us," whispered Hailey. "If that's him in the reeds, I'm gonna take a stick to him."

"Peeping?" Ashley slid from her resting place and joined her sister in the deeper water. "Can't be Noah," she said just above a whisper. "His father's got him breaking ground with his new mule. He'll be busy most of the week."

"See that?" said Hailey as she pointed to the reeds

still moving on the north west side of the pond. It's working its way toward the big, flat rock on the north side."

Now, making little effort to hide its presence, the movements in the eight-foot reeds between them and the big river became more active as the intruder neared the four-foot tall stone barely forty feet from them. But, just as the movement neared the stone, it stopped.

"Go and get our clothes," whispered Ashley.

"Me?" Hailey sank to her nose, slowly shaking her head. "It's a big, black dog. I got a glimpse of it through the reeds and its just waiting to jump up on that rock."

"How about—"

Ashley's suggestion was cut short as Hailey's 'dog' jumped from the reeds to the top of the stone.

"Wolf," said Hailey weakly. "Where did he come from?"

"Where?" echoed Ashley. "The woods are everywhere. The question is, 'Can they hear us dying at the house?'"

"Help!" screamed Hailey.

"The wolf's hackles came up immediately. Growling and snapping his huge, white teeth, he eyed the girls intently.

"Don't do that again," snapped Ashley. "You scared me, and that creature doesn't like it either. One more yell like that and he'll be in here with us."

Hailey squinted at her older sister and then asked, "All right Miss Know-it-all, what should we do next?"

"I have no . . ." Ashley's words faded as she looked to her left and added, "What do you make of that?"

The two sisters eased close to each other as they watched a bright, pulsating object hovering just above the treetops to their left.

"There's someone in it," whispered Ashley. "Look how dark it has become all around us.

"You're right, but I can barely see shape. I can't tell if it's a man or woman. The ball of light is much too bright."

Suddenly, without so much as a whisper, the object

streaked toward the wolf, picked it up, and then carried it whimpering and struggling back out over the river.

The girls sat there for a moment, completely astonished by what they had just seen.

"It took the wolf! It took the wolf!" exclaimed Hailey.

"Come," added Ashley. She took her sister by the arm. "Let's get to the house before either one of them comes back."

"That's it!" exclaimed Hailey as she pulled ahead of her sister. "That bright thing was as scary as the black wolf."

"Just grab 'em!" exclaimed Ashley, noting her sister was pausing at their pile of clothes.

As they ran for the house, Hailey kept checking the woods, but there was no sign of the wolf or the bright object that took him.

"Have you lost your minds?" exclaimed Heather. Their mother stood on the front porch with the back door open. The forty-year-old, strawberry blond slowly crossed her arms, eying the two.

Hailey, upon seeing her, at the door tapping her right foot, slowed abruptly. Ashley, however, all but run her over.

"Keep going!" exclaimed Ashley as she glanced behind her again.

"Girls!" snapped Heather loudly. Then, showing remarkable restraint as the two reached the porch, she calmly added, "Why are you two naked as a jaybird?"

"What?" spoke a familiar voice from the family room.

Russell Nutt, a middle-aged hunter and woodsman, walked toward the kitchen but was stopped before he got to the door.

"Not another step, Russell," warned Heather, glancing back at him. "I've got a situation here if I can just find a handle on it."

Quickly turning from a grinning husband, Heather wheeled around and
hurried back to the door. The girls, barely in their knickers, were scrambling to get their other garments on.

"I'm waiting," said Heather, noting their abnormal interest in the area around the pool.

"A wolf attacked us," replied Hailey, struggling with her blouse. "It was a huge black one."

"He didn't exactly attack us," corrected Ashley as she slipped her dress on. "The wolf got attacked by the something that saved us."

"Wait, wait," said Russell. He walked up behind Heather. "Did it or did it not attack you?"

"Kind of," answered Hailey.

"Not exactly," corrected Ashley again, but it probably would have if that bright thing hadn't taken it away."

"Bright thing? Wolf?" Russell pushed past Heather taking his bow and quiver from the wall. Pausing on the porch, looked back at Heather, and said, "Keep looking for that 'handle'. I'll have a look around the pool." He then looked down at his daughters and asked, "Have you two been eating mushrooms again? I've told you not to pick them unless I'm there."

"We-have-not," assured Ashley

"Then, where was this wolf?"

Hailey quickly pointed toward the north side of the pool. "Right there on that big, flat rock. But it's gone now."

Russell raised his eyebrows. "And just how do we know that?" he asked.

Hailey slowly looked back at Ashley. "You enjoy explaining things. Try this one on for size."

Ashley rolled her eyes, her gaze ending up on her father. "I promise there are no mushrooms involved. The wolf . . ." Her voice trailed off as she looked at her sister.

"Go ahead. You're doing great," encouraged Hailey.

With a deep breath, Ashley continued, "It was taken from us by a big, bright thing that flew in from the trees. It was almost as large as a buggy."

Both Heather and Russell remained silent for a moment. Finally, and in unison, they both said, "Mushrooms!"

"Come in here right now while you father checks

the woods," grumbled Heather. "If you're still hungry, supper will be on the table in half an hour."

"Auugh!" groaned Ashley, but Hailey remained strangely quiet.

* * *

The next evening, along the creek that leads east from the pond, the two sisters worked diligently on one of their ginseng patches where the creek entered the Mississippi River. The April Friday had proved quite warm, and with the weekend well within reach, Hailey could hardly go any farther . . .

"I don't think this patch really needs weeding and mulching," complained Hailey, leaning upon her hoe. "It looks bunches better than when we found it." She looked at a particularly wide part in the creek. "Doesn't that look good to you?" she added, nodding at the calm pool of water. "It's wide and deep enough and it doesn't have a single reed for that wolf to hide in."

Ashley stopped hoeing, glanced at the creek, and then wiped the sweat from her forehead with her right hand. "It does look good," she softly admitted. "Tomorrow's Saturday and we've got at least four hours before dark."

"Let's take a dip and go home." Hailey pulled out a handkerchief from her dress pocket and unwrapped a small piece of rose-colored soap.

"Ohhh my word," said Ashley with a bit of a grin. You've been into mother's trunk.

"Yep, but I left her the brand new bar," quipped Hailey. Grinning, she dropped her hoe and ran for the stream.

"Good enough for me, but keep an eye on the woods," added Ashley as she quickly followed her sister's lead.

After soaping from head to toe, Hailey handed the little, pink bar to her sister.

Ashley did much the same, ending up with suds all over her face and head. As she was working the lather into her hair, her sister poked her lightly on the right arm.

"What?" asked Ashley, pausing with lather all over her face.

"You'd better have a look right now."

Normally, Ashley would have finished washing her face, but the weak tone in her sister's voice made her heart jump. She quickly washed the soap from her face. As she removed her hands, her eyes focused on a pair of old, black shoes with square, brass buckles, and then on the huge, black wolf that was standing next to them.

"I didn't even hear them walk up," whispered Hailey.

"Who are you?" asked Ashley weakly. Being trapped in the wolf's stare, she could hardly look at the old woman.

Clearly well into her seventies, she looked as passive as someone's grandmother.

"Just a neighbor," replied the old woman. She straightened her brown, pocketed apron, which covered the front of her long, black dress. "I'm somewhat angry at what you two meddlers did to my friend, Ferris here, and my little herb patches."

Ashley finally managed to pull her stare away from the wolf and look at the one who was speaking. Her hair was gray, and pulled back tightly in a small bun behind her head. Her eyes were dark, but not unfriendly. Although looking like someone's kindly old grandmother, her tight-lipped smile betrayed her.

"We know our neighbors," replied Ashley, eyeing the wolf again. "I've lived in Inslee Bottoms all my life and I don't remember you at all."

Her tight-lipped smile widened as she said, "I have been ignorantly blissful at not having to deal with you two until you took to harvesting my patches and now attacking my Ferris," she explained leaning heavily on her dark red walking stick.

"What's your name?" asked Hailey. The two sisters struggled for cover in barely three foot of water.

"Laphidius Monks," answered the old woman. "I don't remember feeling the presence of others in the craft roaming about these woods. How is it I missed you two?" she added, leaning heavily forward upon her stick.

"Missed?" Ashley glanced at her sister. "We don't

have a craft."

"You spelled my wolf!" Her eyes squinted. "I've overlooked the pilfering of my mandrake and ginseng patches, but the spelling of my familiar I cannot abide. That deed bears a price."

"We did nothing to your animal," explained Hailey. "He was at our pond yesterday, but what took him from us I can only describe."

"Not interested in your lies," snapped Laphidius. "I saw, from a distance, the spell that brought him to me," she added as she stepped close to the water's edge.

She extended her walking stick to a stone at the creek's edge. When it touched it, blue sparks flew as if steel striking flint causing the girls to flinch.

She then spoke in the form of a rhyme:

Now in the water,
The spell will tarry,
Until these two
Are small as faeries.

Newid Cerewid!" she said loudly. The girls flinched again.

"It did it again," said Hailey. She rubbed her face with her hands. "I'm tingling all over."

Leaving the two with a maniacal grin on her old, wrinkled fade, the old woman walked back into the woods with her wolf.

"I don't know that old woman," said Ashley, also rubbing arms and face. "She didn't even ask our names or . . ." her voice faded below a whisper as she looked about the creek. "The water's getting deeper, Hailey. I can barely touch the bottom."

"The bank! Look at the bank!" shouted Hailey as the two struggled to stay afloat. "I can't swim that far. She's done something to the creek."

"Not true, foolish human," spoke someone directly above Hailey.

Before either of them could look up, strong hands grabbed them by the hair.

"Stop struggling and we'll get you to the bank!"

spoke a soft but determined voice.

Try as she did, Hailey couldn't turn to see her sister or the one who was helping her. The air quickly became full of wind and a strange humming started as if some giant bee was above her. When her feet finally touched the muddy bottom close to the bank, she grabbed the first thing she could see. It was a shoot of grass the size of a corn stalk.

"Get out of the water! Get to our clothes!" exclaimed Ashley as she pushed her sister through the tall grass and away from the bank.

"Not so loud," complained Hailey. She paused, staring at a huge mound of linen in front of them.

"I don't think they'll fit," said a male voice directly behind them.

As Ashley dove into the mound of clothes, Hailey sat down in the heap, covered herself, and then looked toward the flat stone where she heard the voice.

"They have wings," whispered Ashley, peeping from under what now looked to be a huge, blue sheet-of-a-dress.

"They are as big as we are and all boys," added Hailey, pulling the linens closer to her.

A round of laughter erupted from the stone as several 'winged' people crowded to its edge.

"Not so," one finally said. "You are as 'small as we are' would be the correct observation, I would say."

"Let's go home," pleaded Hailey. "Mom and Dad will know what to do."

Ashley rolled her eyes and replied, "Are you kidding? We're ten times as small as we were. That means we're ten times as far from home and it's almost dark. We'll never make it. Something's bound to pounce on us."

This caused another round of laughter from those on the stone.

"Off the rock! Into the forest with you!" shouted someone near the boulder where the boy faes were standing.

Then, as the girls watched the faeries leave the

stone, the air all around them became full of that same humming sound that accompanied their rescue. As they tried to look past the clothes, another faerie shot over and landed directly in front of them. She looked to be about their age and was dressed completely in green, except for a black, moleskin hat. Her long, russet-colored hair was pulled back in a ponytail and tied with a black ribbon.

"In trouble, huh?" asked the fae. Her smile seemed more sympathetic than spiteful.

"Who are you?" asked Ashley, noting the girl fae seemed to be looking them over.

"Ohhhh she really did a number on you two didn't she?" replied the little fae. Finally, noting the desperation in their faces, she added, "I'm Rosebud. I live in Kiendom, but you two are from the cabin just north of the spring. Have you figured your rescuer out yet? If so, what do you think the bright object was?"

Ashley and Hailey, mostly speechless, remained content to listen to the tearing and rending of material coming from the far side of the heap they were sitting in.

"We don't know what it was," replied Ashley finally. "What has just happened has completely astounded us."

"I suppose so," giggled Rosebud, "but I think that bright whatever is the key to relieving your problem right now--getting out of the Witch's spell that is."

Ashley slowly shook her head. "I'm quite sure we would have no idea what it was, but we'll gladly take any help we can right now."

The little, green-clothed fae smiled, looking closely at the two still huddled in their over-sized clothes.

"The bright object you saw was a concentration of light around a being you two were probably never aware of," she explained softly. "You would have seen what he was riding, had he not been for the light."

"Riding?" Hailey slowly leaned closer to the little fae. "We weren't aware it was riding anything actually."

"It was a dragon," replied Rosebud.

"Dragon?" said Hailey weakly.

"The Great Naught," replied Rosebud as the tearing and ripping continued behind the mound of clothes.

"You're putting us on, aren't you?" asked Ashley.

"What kind of man could ride such a thing?"

"A half elf and all Wizard blessed with an unusually long lifetime," answered Rosebud. "He's got the ability to gather about him light so dense that most everything else close to him would appear as night. That's when the dragon comes . . . in the night part."

"You're putting us on again, aren't you?" echoed Ashley.

"Try putting this on," said another voice as two dresses were tossed over their heads to land in front of them.

As the two girls looked on, another girl faerie landed beside Rosebud. She looked a bit older--forties as the world of men would judge age. She was dressed in brown and had short brown hair. It was frizzed in more directions than a sane person could count.

"I see mine," exclaimed Hailey. She grabbed the purple dress and then handed the blue one to her sister.

"My name is Lilly Ann," said the fae dressed in the brown shades of winter.

"I'm Ashley Nutt." Then, as her head popped out of her garment's neck hole, she nodded at her sister and added, "She's my sister, Hailey. What about this Wizard thing?"

"That would be Mangus Terellus," answered Lilly Ann. "He's been gone now for at least thirty years. I expect him to be an old man by now. But if the Great Naught is alive, then he must be as well."

Ashley stood, straightening her dress, and then asked, "Where does he live?"

"No idea," confessed Lilly Ann, "but it must be close since we saw him at your pool. The gnomish Wizard Yenwolk Stonesmith might know, but he's way up at the Whitestone Castle."

"Ben Terry," suggested Rosebud weakly.

Lilly Ann looked at her for a moment and then smiled. "That just might work." She quickly turned to the two half-lings. "Yenwolk sometimes confides in Old Ben."

"Wait a minute," said Ashley. "I know him—short, gray hair, fuzzy beard, and a bushy mustache."

Ashley nodded. "But he lives north of the dwarf village of Leachenwood. That's a good bit from our home."

"I'll fix that," said the brown fae.

She wheeled on her heels, and flew away, disappearing into the shadows of the forest.

"Awww nuts. Not the Frost Owl again," complained Rosebud. Lolling her hear around toward the woods, she shouted, "Why not Feathersfoot?"

"Too small," said a little fae dressed in yellow. She was watching atop the mound of clothes with her friends. "Besides," she added laughing, "the Frost Owl won't bite you again if you get rid of that moleskin cap."

"I'll dust these two," said Rosebud. She pulled out a deerskin pouch from a little bag dangling by a strap on her shoulders. "Close your eyes. This will make you a bit lighter."

The air quickly became full of yellow, blue, and green, sparkling dust.

"What's that glittering stuff?" asked Hailey as she began to sneeze.

"Levastadt," replied Rosebud. "It'll make you light as a feather. Less strain on Lilly Ann's old owl."

"What's the Frost Owl?" asked Ashley. "Do we really ride him?"

"Hmmm," mused Rosebud for a moment. "He's a night predator, but I don't want to scare you. He hunts the Frost Forests way north of here at Snow Lake in the winter. But he stays with us during the warmer months. When he comes in, just stay close to me."

"But he bit you once," said Ashley with a bit of squint.

"Yes . . ." Rosebud quickly pulled her cap off and stuffed it inside her bag. "That was my fault."

"He still won't be happy when Lilly Ann wakes him," said the yellow fae. "He prefers the night, and they're still humans you know."

"Awww nuts," said Rosebud again as she glanced toward where Lilly Ann had flown. She opened the drawstrings of her bag, fished around, and finally pulled out a little wooden jar with a cork top. Handing it out to Ashley, she said, "Rub this all over you two. That'll fool him . . . I hope."

Ashley quickly pulled the stopper and peered inside at the thick, yellow cream. "Honeysuckle," she said with a bit of a grin.

"Put it everywhere," said the yellow fae. "If he smells human, you'll be in a fix."

Then, as Hailey had her turn at the honeysuckle jar, a shrill scream echoed from high in the trees.

"There they are," exclaimed Ashley as she pointed a shaky finger up the creek. "Have mercy," she added just above a whisper. "I didn't know an owl could look so big."

"It's a Great Horned," said the yellow fae. "If you make a friend of him, you will benefit from it I think."

Although Hailey didn't say a word, she quickly eased close to Rosebud and pulled Ashley with her.

Huge leaves flew from the ground like bed sheets before a thunderstorm as the huge russet and white creature landed just paces from them. He first looked at Rosebud, then at Ashley, but when he spotted Hailey, his gaze froze on the half-ling.

"More cream," whispered Rosebud.

"Come around! Come around!" shouted Lilly Ann as she pulled at the feathers on the left side of his neck.

Finally, about the time Hailey found the bottom of the honeysuckle jar, the old owl presented his right side and promptly sat in the grass.

"Get on quick," replied Lilly Ann. As she flew up beside Lilly Ann, she added, "He's not exactly pleased with this.

"Take my hands," Rosebud told them as she quickly grabbed the girls. "I'll take you to his back behind us."

"Ohhh my gosh!" Ashley held tight as she was pulled form the ground.

Hailey winced at the volume in her sister's voice, but could find little breath to complain.

"We will hold to this," directed Lilly Ann. She held up a crimson rope lying across the great owl's shoulders. "You two sit behind us and hold on to our belts.

"But," started Hailey.

"It'll be easy," interrupted Lilly Ann, noticing the

girls were hesitating a bit.

Hailey eyed the satchel Rosebud held close to her side. All her life she had heard about levistadt, the magical faerie dust. Now it was right in front of her.

"We'll head toward Leachenwood," said Lilly Ann, "and then north along the Whitestone River."

Rosebud looked back at the half-lings and whispered, "Woodland Faes seldom scream. If you don't want the Frost Owl to take a closer look at you, be as quiet as you possibly can." She nodded at Lilly Ann.

With one shrill whistle from Lilly Ann, the Frost Owl crouched and leaped into the air. With but four, powerful strokes, he was well atop the trees and heading in a northerly direction.

"I can't believe it," declared Ashley. "Holding on is much easier than I thought, and . . ." Pausing for a moment, she looked at her sister. "Get your face out of the feathers and look at what's happening," she said loudly.

"I think I'm going to be sick," groaned Hailey.

"The October air is cool," said Rosebud looking back at Hailey. "Get your face into it and it'll help dispel the feeling."

"There's the steam column rising from Leachenwood's cave," said Lilly Ann, pointing out ghostly, white clouds drifting up into the night skies.

"Don't miss the creek," warned Rosebud. "I don't want to get lost when night is this close."

"Look at that," said Ashley, nudging her sister.

A single column of steam and smoke the width of a pine tree was slowly rising from a hole atop a huge, smooth, rounded stone. Clearly visible above the treetops, the blanched, granite object stood out like a beacon in the late evening.

"Is that where the dwarves live?" asked Hailey weakly.

"Yes," answered Rosebud. "Below that white skullcap are three levels of homes. They raise mushrooms, truffles, turnips, pumpkins, mandrakes, and the cutest, little, furry horses you've ever seen."

"You'll meet one of the dwarves today," added Lilly

Ann. "His name is Grimm, but don't be fooled by a name. You'll like him. He's funny."

Hailey slowly raised her head a bit more and watched the moonlit treetops slide beneath them as if in a dream. Then, glittering here and there, something bright on the ground seemed to be following them.

Noticing she was following the object from one side of the owl to the other, Rosebud laughed and then replied, "It's the moon. Its reflection follows the Whitestone creek as we do. Watch close," she added, "I think I see chimney smoke from the far side of the next hill. That will be where Old Ben lives."

As the Frost Owl neared the top of the hill, Rosebud noted that Lilly Ann had an uncommon interest in something behind them. "What's bothering you?" Rosebud finally asked.

"I think we're being followed—a raven I think."

"The Wizard Yenwolk has a raven," replied Rosebud. "His name is Soot."

"Soot's not that big," added Lilly Ann with a quick, backward glance. "I think it's Cochi."

Rosebud, almost letting go of the tether, quickly spun around. "Nooo you don't," she said weakly.

"Who is Cochi?" asked Ashley.

"It's not a 'who'," answered Rosebud, now all but obsessed with black skies above them. "It's Laphidius' other familiar, or that is, her pet. That Witch's got an uncommon interest in what we're doing," she mumbled as she slowly faced forward.

Lilly Ann slowly shook her head as she added, "No one ever knows what a witch will do. Perhaps she's still gloating on what she's done to these half-lings."

"There it is," exclaimed Rosebud as the Frost Owl topped the last hill. "Two lines of smoke. He's cooking something and I'm so hungry I could eat the stubbles off of the witch's broom."

Lilly Ann leaned closer to the Great Owl's head. "Go down, great one. Go down," she said loudly.

With its huge, gray and white wings stretch out, the massive hunter glided in as silent as a snowflake on a calm night. Gliding around one tree after another, it finally came to a small clearing with a log cabin on the far side.

Quickly approaching the cabin, Lilly Ann stood on her knees and leaned heavily on the Frost Owl's neck. "To the grass, great one! To the grass!" she said loudly.

"Hold on!" exclaimed Rosebud. "He won't get much closer and sometimes he doesn't land very well."

Hailey, glancing at Ashley, tightening her grip on Rosebud's belt and then tried to get a glimpse of what was ahead of them. A blur of russet, hewn pine shingles and a huge front porch was all she could manage before the Frost Owl wheeled to his left in a tight spiral.

"Ohhh help!" screamed Hailey as her legs slipped from the creature's back. With her feet now touching the owl's right wing, it was all she could do to hold on to Rosebud's belt. "Rosebud!" she shouted.

Rosebud, struggling with her grip on the tether, quickly reached out for the half-ling, but all she could come up with was a handful of coal-black hair. "Don't scream," warned the faerie. She pushed Hailey's head down into the owl's feathers. Then, in a flurry of leaves, pine needles, and grass, the Frost Owl landed with bone jarring thump, sending Hailey sliding off the back of its wing and into the waist-high grass.

Hailey immediately scrambled to her feet and stood there, red-faced and tight-fisted. "What the devil was that," she exclaimed," pushing the grass from before her, she glared at Rosebud. "You pulled my hair."

"Distract your owl," said Rosebud. She then flew to Hailey's side as the others dismounted.

Try as she did, Lilly Ann had no luck with the creature. As Ashley was sliding from its back, the huge, black-eyed predator wheeled and slowly walked toward the two in the grass.

"Don't run. Whatever you do, don't run," said Rosebud as they backed from the grass and onto a protruding root of a white oak tree.

The Frost Owl stopped just a breath away from the two, lowered its face down close to Hailey, and then stopped still, snapping its huge, curved beak.

“Point up and shout fly,” whispered Rosebud.

Hailey, with her eyebrows up to her hairline and stiff as a board, said nothing as the great owl got closer and closer to her face.

Then, from somewhere behind the tree they were standing on, someone shouted, “Shoo!”

Immediately, in a maze of flying grass, leaves, faeries, and half-lings, the huge Great Horned Owl scrambled from the grass and bounded into the air.

“Great horny toads!” exclaimed Lilly Ann as she chose to fly up into the white oak instead of being bowled over, or blown away like the other three.

Ashley, desperately clinging to a limb six feet from the ground, looked about for the others, and whatever had scared the owl off. Suddenly, she felt the ground beneath her feet again. Knowing this just couldn’t be possible, she looked down.

A huge hand? she thought as her heart began to pound and race.

“Turn loose. You won’t fall,” spoke a voice below her. The tone seemed kind and friendly.

Looking over her left shoulder and down a bit, she saw a short, stocky man with a big, bulbous nose. The smile in his big, blue eyes echoed the one trying to escape his bushy, red mustache.

“I like your red hair,” replied Ashley weakly, noting the smile was still there.

“It’s a pain sometimes, but I’m too lazy to cut it. Besides, I can’t see the back of my head.

“Grimm!” exclaimed Rosebud happily as she and Lilly Ann dug Hailey from under the leaves.

“Having trouble with your familiar, ‘Little One’. Looks like you four could use some landin’ lessons.” Still holding his hand under Ashley, the dwarf waited for Lilly Ann’s reply.

“He’s not my familiar,” she finally snapped. “He’s my friend and I raised him from a wee peeper.”

“That you did,” he exclaimed through a hearty laugh, holding his rotund belly. He looked back at Ashley. “Come now. Turn loose,” he added through a chuckle, “I haven't got all day after all."

"Very well then," replied Ashley weakly. She released the limb and promptly fell to his palm.

The dwarf then bent down and sat the half-ling in the grass beside the others. Looking closely at the two sisters, he said softly, "By my Great Aunt Hattie's birthmark, where are your wings?"

"That's why we're here," answered Lilly Ann. "Is Ben Terry home?"

"He is, and he's doctoring up a fine, beef stew. I know you fae folk aren't too keen on beef, but--"

"We are!" exclaimed the half-lings.

"You are?" asked the dwarf as he rubbed the underside of his nose with his right index finger.

"That's why we're here also," explained Rosebud. "They're humankind. Laphidius spelled them."

"No-she-did-not," spoke the dwarf in disbelief. Looking closely at the half-lings he added, "What are your names?"

"I'm Ashley Nutt." Ashley then nodded at her sister and added, "She's my sister, Hailey."

"Well, I'm Bonfed Grimm. You can just call me Grimm. I've been scrounging for nuts and mushrooms," he explained as he picked up a coarsely woven basket behind him. "Here," he added as he placed the basket in front of the four, "This beats flying or walking to Old Ben's house."

"That'll work," replied Rosebud happily. She grabbed Ashley's arm and carried her up and over the side of the basket.

"I've never seen mushrooms so big," said Ashley as she promptly broke off a small piece. Then, as Lilly Ann helped Hailey into the 'free ride', she gently pushed at one of the watermelon-sized pecans.

"Hold on now," spoke Grimm as he picked up the basket.

Hailey eased up to the side of the basket for another look at where they were going. The cabin was made of pine slats and sported a wide porch that spanned all the way across the front. There were two chimneys; one was on the left side and the other more in the middle of the cabin. The one in the middle was smoking heavily and smelled of oak wood. Light was coming from the two windows to the right of the front door, but the rest of the cabin was strangely dark.

Grimm quickly stepped to the front porch, pulled on the heavy latch to the door, and then pushed it open with a squeak-popping sound. Pausing, he watched an old fellow who was bent over an iron pot. It was swung over the fire suspended on a movable iron rod. From what could be seen, his hair was gray and thinned, almost to the point of balding, over five feet tall, but not even close to six, and a bit overweight.

"Ohhh wow," said Ashley as warm air laced with the smell of fresh beef stew floated by her face.

Hailey scrambled across the huge pecans to the front of the basket. Obviously a family place, the room alone was half as big as their own cabin with padded couches, chairs, and a big, oval table a bit to the right of the center of the room. The door on the right side of it was closed.

Probably a bedroom she thought.

But the door to the left of it was open and appeared to be a cupboard or storage room. It contained numerous baskets labeled dried apples, potatoes, tree bark, herbs, and mandrakes. Glass jars lined the windowsill and were full of many colored things the contents of which one could only imagine. Below the window was a huge basket full of abalone shells and giant tree lichens. To the right of it, was seven-foot carving of something that made her flinch—a black dragon, complete with white fangs and an impressive set of white, backward-curved horns.

"Got somethin' for ya," said Grimm. He stepped inside and closed the door.

"Good," said Old Ben. Glancing back at the basket of nuts and mushrooms, he added, "Wash em' and we'll have em' for supper."

"Ha!" exclaimed the dwarf loudly as he walked to the table on his right and set the basket down in front of a huge, padded couch of brown leather. It looked to be as old as the man stirring the stew. The dwarf then turned to face the old fellow and added, “I don’t think that would set well with ‘em, Sir.”

“What did you say?” asked the old fellow softly. He turned with a big, wooden spoon in his right hand. His short beard was almost as white as his gray hair, and neatly trimmed.

With the spoon dripping on the hearth, he just stared at the basket.

Grimm cleared his throat, straightened his checked vest, and then said, “They need your help, Sir.” Gesturing toward the basket with his right thumb as he added, “It seems Laphidius is back again and has had at the wingless ones. They’re humankind they are.”

“You-don’-say,” he replied weakly as he dropped the spoon to the hearth and paused for a moment. “Human?” he then exclaimed as he picked up the spoon and tossed it into the pot. Walking briskly to the basket, he looked closely at Ashley and Hailey.

“They are,” assured Lilly Ann. “Whitestone is such a distance and--”

The faerie’s explanation was cut short by the snapping of front door’s latch. Grimm started for the door but only took a couple of steps when it quickly swung open. The dwarf stopped in his tracks, staring at a smile upon an old woman’s face.

“Laphidius Monks,” he said just above a whisper.

Wearing the same brown, pocketed apron, she still had the kindly, old grandmother look, but now a smile to go with it.

“Hello, Grimm,” she said politely, barely looking at Old Ben. The dwarf slowly backed toward the basket, glancing at Old Ben as he did so. “Aren’t you going to invite me in?”

Rosebud and Lilly Ann, instantly jumped over the far side of the basket and dropped down behind it. Hailey and Ashley remained content to just peep through its woven, cane strips.

Remaining in the doorway, she slowly looked to Old Ben.

“Ben Terry, are you still alive?” she asked as she stepped just inside the doorway and then paused, leaning heavily on her dark red walking stick.

"Yes." He walked over to the iron kettle, picked up the wooden spoon, looked back at her, and then added, "I see that you are still much the same as I remembered."

"What do you know of me, old man?" she grumbled. "I've seen you only twice in the last twenty years." She looked toward the basket. Noting the half lings peeping over the edge, she laughed silently. "I see your little bath in the stream took off more than usual, little ones. Perhaps next time you'll stay away from my wolf and woodland patches as well."

"They looked wild to me," explained Ashley. "We only weeded and cultivated them."

"For the taking," mumbled the Witch. Stepping closer, she paused, awaiting Old Ben's reaction.

"Terribly presumptuous of you, Laphidius," said Ben, never turning from his pot.

Grim immediately backed from in front of the oval table and closer to the basket. Never taking his eyes off the witch, he slid the basket close to his side. Rosebud and Lilly Ann hustled to keep behind the basket and away from Laphidius' attention.

"Look," whispered Hailey. She pointed to the storage room. "The black statue is gone."

"What statue?" asked Ashley.

Rosebud and Lilly Ann quickly looked toward where Hailey was pointing. "Ohhhh, this is not good," groaned Lilly Ann. "Ben's going to do something drastic, and the only way out of here is way too close to the Witch.

Laphidius then slowly looked from the basket and back to Old Ben. "I care not about being presumptuous, Ben Terry." She eyed his back still to her. "I go where I please, to do what I feel needs be done."

The old fellow released the spoon to plop back in the stew, straightened up, and then stretched his back with a grimace. Then, like he had all the time in the world, he reached to the set of deer antlers mounted above the mantle and took down a maroon, yellow-grained staff which was resting upon them. Turning back to face the Witch, he placed the base of the staff gently upon the floor.

The Witch's eyes opened wide as her chin dropped slightly. "The staff of Ghorumm," she whispered. The look of confidence quickly faded from her expression. "I should have noticed that when I came in. Where did you come by that?" she added, now gripping her walking stick with both hands.

Old Ben stepped from the hearth, stopped, and then said, "For all these past years, I've lived in blissful anonymity. Who would think the antics of an old crone would bring that to an end?"

The Witch's eyes grew even bigger as she looked past the old man's beard and mustache. "Magnus Terellis," she said weakly as she started backing toward the door. "I mean neither harm nor disrespect here," she added, almost calmly as she stopped just inside the doorway.

"Well, the cat's out of the bag," whispered Lilly Ann. "I guess Old Ben's peaceful days are at an end."

Peaceful days?" echoed Hailey. "What do you mean?"

"The Bright Rider returns," whispered Rosebud. "Just watch the wooden fist on the head of his staff. When it opens, be ready to duck."

"As the two half-lings watched the fist slowly open, Old Ben spoke a charm:

"Come, vision of shadows,
Essence of Meld,
And take this crone far
From the half-lings she's spelled."

"Here it comes," said Rosebud. She quickly ducked down on the table behind the basket and closed her eyes.

Seeing this, Ashley and Hailey quickly looked at Lilly Ann, but she seemed as if frozen--mouth open and eyes wide. Her gaze transfixed on the area just outside the doorway. It was growing strangely dim.

"What's happening?" whispered Ashley to Lilly Ann as the two half-lings knelt down in the basket.

"The Great Naught comes," said the fae just above a whisper.

Now, blocked by a powerful wizard within the cabin

and cut off by what she knew was waiting in the darkness behind her, Laphidius' eyes grew wide with fear.

"Look at that," whispered Lilly Ann as a black, tentacle-shaped arm eased through the doorway and wound itself about the old woman's waist.

Laphidius, seemingly in shock, moved not an inch. "Mangus, call him off," she shouted.

But even as she screamed out the words, she was lifted from the floor and pulled from the doorway.

Raising his staff, Ben said, "Kom Toppae!"

"He calls the witch's stick," whispered Lilly Ann.

The walking stick twisted free of the old woman and flew to Ben's outstretched left hand.

Without so much as a parting word, Laphidius was taken from the doorway and out into the darkness.

"Has he got her stick?" asked Rosebud, now peeping through her fingers.

"He does," answered Lilly Ann. "You can open your eyes and get up now."

Rosebud stood quickly, checked the door, and then flew straightway to the nearest window. "Come see! Come see!" she exclaimed, jumping up and down on its sill.

Grimm quickly picked up the basket as Lilly Ann jumped in and then walked briskly toward the window. Old Ben, simply replaced the staff to the deer antlers and went back to stirring his stew.

"Ohhh my Goodness," said Hailey weakly as Grimm held the basket next to the window. "I can see the creature's wings as it nears the moon. The witch is hanging from its shadow-like tail like a mouse tangled in woodbine. It's taking her toward the river."

Ashley quickly wiped the moist window with her sleeve and then pushed her nose against its cold pane. Even from a considerable distance, she could make out the creature's curved horns and bat-like wings as it soared across the moon's full, yellow face.

"I'm very sorry, Sir," said Grimm as he moved the basket from the window. "I didn't really know she was following the half-lings.

"Well . . ." sighed Ben Terry, "I don't think

Laphidius will tell anyone. The Naught will make it quite plain the penalties of disclosing such a thing. She certainly will not get past them." He glanced at those in the basket, but said nothing.

"They need your help, Ben Terry," said Lilly Ann. "Laphidius spelled them with her stick."

"A fair price would be their silence," suggested Rosebud. She flew from the windowsill and lit by the basket on the table.

"We'll say nothing, Sir. Just please help us get home," said Ashley as Hailey nodded her approval.

"That's comforting," said Ben. He looked at the Witch's stick and asked, "A static spark from the base of this instrument loosed the spell did it not?"

"It did, Sir," assured Hailey. "We both felt the tingle while still in the water."

Ben turned and walked to the center of the room still holding the Witch's stick. "Grim," he said, looking closely at the stick, "place the half-lings before me. Lilly Ann, you can join Rosebud on the table."

"Out of the way, little faes," said Grimm. He picked up two blankets from a nearby couch, laid one upon the floor and placed the other one beside it.

"I get it," explained Rosebud as Grim picked up the basket and placed it between the blankets. "When Ben brings the light, they will grow to their own size and right out of their clothes."

"Exactly," said Grim as he shooed the two half lings from the basket with a swish of his hands. "Now, each of you pick a blanket. Get under it, and hold to its edge. If everything goes correctly, you'll soon loose your knickers."

"Will it hurt," asked Ashley, noting Lilly Ann's haste to leave them.

"A bit unpleasant perhaps, but a small price to pay for normality I would say. Now, shut your eyes if you like."

As the half-lings closed their eyes, Old Ben recited a spell of his own:

"From the Witch's stick
I now shatter the spell

Which even now
In these half-lings doth dwell."

"Holliock!" he shouted loudly, tapping the stick on the wooden floor.

"Nothing . . . not a spark," said Rosebud. "Strike the stick a bit harder, Sir."

Ben did as the fae suggested, but, still, nothing happened.

"Afraid this would happen." Ben scratched his head and then smoothed back his thinning hair. "She's spelled the stick against all magic but her own."

Hailey quickly looked up at the old man. "But we can't stay like this forever. What can we do?"

Ben smiled, replying, "Against pure light all evil flees." He cast the stick to Grimm and added, "Break it up and put it in the fire where it belongs."

As Grimm broke up the Witch's stick, the old Wizard took his staff back down from the rack.

"Uh oh," said Rosebud again. The two faes eased close to the half-lings. "Here we go again."

"Shut the door, shutter the windows, and turn the lamps up as high as they will go," he instructed.

"I'll get the lamps, Grimm." Lilly Ann flew from the basket.

Rosebud whispered. "The spell of Gathering comes. He'll gather the light close to us and we'll want to be with you when it comes."

Lilly Ann shot back to the blanket so fast she actually stumbled upon landing. "First sign of the Bright Rider in thirty years she said excitedly. "Don't move a muscle."

"This scares the devil out of me," whispered Ashley. She looked at the two faes. "Please, tell me what he's going to do."

"Nothing to harm you. Just driving evil from this place. Just shield your eyes from the light if you must."

"No guarantees," said Ben, "but it's still worth a try." He then spoke a much different spell:

"Now with rays of uncommon clarity,
Dispel this evil with utmost brevity.
Gather to me from my humble room
And banish the evil from the Witch's tome.

Kom Toppae!" he shouted loudly.

Rosebud crouched close to Hailey. "A tome is a big book," she explained. "He refers to Laphidius' Book of Shadows."

"He just called the light," added Lilly Ann.

Ever so slowly, little by little, the light dimmed as it formed a glowing path from each lamp straight to Old Ben. The glowing matter began to swirl all about him. Even the fireplace began to lose its glow toward the old gentleman, causing the flames to burn with a strange, dark blue hue."

"Here it comes," said Rosebud with raised eyebrows.

As the faes and half lings shielded her eyes, the streaks of light bonded as one, glowing orb from Old Ben's feet to the top of his head. He then stepped to the edge of the blanket and knelt by those thereon.

"My word!" exclaimed Hailey, sending the faes scrambling from the blanket. The now growing girls scrambled for their own piece of cover.

"It worked!" exclaimed the faes in unison.

Suddenly, the room was filled with laughter and applause from above them.

"What's this?" grumbled Grimm as he looked up toward the rafter beams of the old cabin. But he could see not a thing for every spark of glow in the whole room was now around the old Wizard.

"*De crescendo*," said Ben softly as he stood.

The glow, as though embarrassed to be so close to a human, shot from him in every direction. With such speed and brightness it caused all in the room to duck to the floor, save for the old Wizard.

The laughter and applause exploded again as Grimm struggled to his feet. "Away with you," he said as he hurried to open the front door.

"Calm yourself, old friend said Ben. They're hurting not one here."

Now, holding their blanket snugly about them, the girls searched the rafters for who the old Wizard was referring to.

"There's hundreds of them," said Hailey. "Their clothes are every color in the rainbow.

"Little pests," grumbled Grimm.

"Now, now," said Ben with a slight chuckle.

"They're hurting not a thing," said Rosebud. "It's been such a long time since they've seen a wizard work, let alone a Bright Rider. Can't they stay?"

The room grew stone quiet as Ben looked about the rafters. "I suppose we've stew and bread enough for them as well, Grimm," said Ben. "Fetch me the small saucers and set the table, but watch them with the wine and honey."

"Very well, Sir," agreed the dwarf, reluctantly.

Lilly Ann then cleared her throat loudly. As Ben looked at her, she nodded toward the girls.

"Ohhh yes. We must not forget our guests of honor. You can go to my room. Lying upon the bed are two sets of Grimm's trousers and shirts. He laid them out for just this occasion."

"Fantastic!" exclaimed Ashley as the two girls shuffled toward the bedroom. Stopping just short of the door, Ashley turned and asked, "How are we to get home from here?"

"Grimm will take you in his wagon tomorrow," replied Ben. "I know your family must be worried, but it's much safer to travel in the light of morning than in the dark of night. Ben looked over his shoulder to where Grimm was hustling around the table. The little faes were already lining up on the far side of it, eying the dwarf suspiciously. "Hurry on now, girls," he added. "We have a whole pot of stew to eat."

* * *

That night, sunk down in Grimm's goose-down, feather bed, Hailey listened to the dwarf snoring from the couch in the adjoining family room. Although the faes were supposed to be gone, at times she could still hear faint sounds of something scurrying about the living room in spite of Ashley's occasional attempt to mimic Grimm's snoring. As if that wouldn't be enough, there were sounds also coming from the storage room on the other side of the wall next to their bed. That occasional thump-dragging sound of something trying to walk should've kept anyone up at night. Yet, everyone seemed to be asleep except her. Finally, the noise just became too much to be ignore. Sliding her feet from the quilt, and to the cold, wood floor, she crept toward the door.

The thump-dragging sound came again. Overcome with curiosity, she continued to the partially open, bedroom door, and peeped out. Old Ben's door was closed. That was good, and she could only see the top of the dwarf's head under a mound of quilts on the couch to the right of the door. Hailey eased the door open and crept out. Just as she passed the couch, the strange sound from the storage room came again, just like someone dragging something across the floor a short distance and then stopping.

Hailey, don't go into that room. The little voice in her head kept repeating. But with Old Ben's door closed and Grimm out cold, her curiosity won out.

More of a pantry, she thought. She gently pushed the door open and eyed the kegs of dried apples, grapes, and plums. *Ohhh boy. It's dessert time.* Lifting the already loose top of a keg marked dried plums, she promptly picked one up and tested it between her thumb and forefinger. *Ripe and sweet.* She thought as she popped it into her mouth.

After picking out a handful, munched on them as she continued to look about the ten-foot square room. Everything was much more organized than her bedroom. The shelves were dusted, canisters and kegs were placed neatly around and close to the walls, and even the windows seemed freshly cleaned. Then, as she chewed on her plums, she caught a glimpse of something on the right side of the window, stuck up in the dark of the corner.

"Wow," whispered Hailey. She tiptoed across the room toward the seven-foot, black statue. "Someone shoved you into that old, cold corner didn't they, mister," she said softly, stopping at arm's length from what looked to be a black dragon. "Certainly look more friendly up close." She looked up at its face.

With chin up, its white-rimmed, yellow eyes seemed to be staring right across the room at the open door. His pointed ears were directly behind his eyes and curved upward and under his two, long, white horns. Ever so slowly, she extended her right hand to touch his onyx-like claws on his left forehand. Just as she did, something moved on the floor in front of her feet. It made the same noise that had so puzzled her from the bedroom. But she wasn't in her bed right now. She quickly stepped back a bit and then looked down. The dragon's feet were hidden by a serpentine tail, which was coiled tightly around them.

"Strange," she whispered.

But as she looked back up, she all but stopped breathing. Instead of seeing the underside of its lower jaw, she was now looking directly into its huge, yellow eyes. His jaw was now resting upon his chest.

"Ohhh-my-Gosh," she said weakly as she noticed his eyes shift from her hands to her face.

With her heart beating like a troll's drum, she slowly backed toward the doorway. As she did, the head of what she thought was a statue, followed her. But the dragon made neither a sound nor any other movement.

"Naught?" she finally managed to say just as her right hand touched the doorframe.

Without another word, she spun around and ran from the room, past Grimm and his couch, and then leaped over the footboard landing next to her sister.

"What?" exclaimed Ashley as she quickly sat up, trying to rub the drowsiness from her face.

"It's back! It's back!" exclaimed Hailey, trying to be as quiet as her excitement would allow.

"What's back? What are you talking about?" Her sister asked sleepily.

"We saw it take the Witch across the moon. The Naught! The Great Naught! It's back in the pantry!"

Ashley glared at her sister through squinted eyes.

"It's right on the far side of that wall," added Hailey, now shaking a nervous finger at the wall.

“Now you’ve done it,” grumbled Ashley. “I’ll never go back to sleep.”

“Would you two like to change beds?” came a loud voice as the bed was soundly bumped.

“Geeze!” exclaimed Hailey as she spun around, ending up on her pillow. “We thought you were asleep,” she added sheepishly.

“Well-I’m-not-now,” he snapped. “What I am is AWAKE! If I hear another peep out of you two half-lings, I’ll have that ‘Dark Terror’ in the next room take you two to Gossimer Swamp. Maybe Laphidius will share somethin’ with you, but I’m sure it won’t be a bed. Now go to sleep!” He wheeled and shuffled his long nightshirt from the room.

“Get under these covers and be quiet,” said Ashley. “And don’t get out of bed again until you hear Grimm get up.”

* * *

That morning, Hailey was awakened by another, strange sound—the whinnying of horses. Slowly, raising up and looking at her sister still asleep, she eased her bare feet to the cold hardwood floor again, slipped from the bed, and then tiptoed to the window. Her eyes immediately grew big as she watched the dwarf hitch up two of the tiniest, fuzziest horses she had ever seen. They stood about waist high, were chocolate-brown, and had long manes. Their tails almost touched the ground.

“Get up! Get up!” she exclaimed as she ran to the bed and shook it.

Ashley immediately scooted up to the headboard, holding a pillow out in front of her like a shield. “Is it in the room? Is it in the room?” she asked loudly.

“No, of course not. Come and look at what Grimm is working with. They’re dwarf horses with a strange, little buggy, and we get to ride in it.”

“Home!” Ashley kicked the quilts off, bounded from the bed, and then peered out of the window. “Ohhh wow!” She ran back and grabbed her oversized, but a bit short, trousers from the foot of the bed. “I’ve never seen a buggy like that one; the driver faces forward and the two benches in the back face each other.”

"Get dressed, girls," said Ben loudly as he knocked on the door. "I've got oat porridge, fried bread, and sausages on the stove. Don't want to send you home hungry."

"Get dressed," said Ashley, fidgeting with the rope in the belt loops of her loose pants. "The quicker we eat, the faster we'll get home."

* * *

In little time, Grimm had the girls in the buggy, and coaxing the little horses down the narrow, rutted trail through the woods.

"This goes to the Whitestone Trail," explained Grimm. "Your place is not that far from where they meet. You're just west of Leachenwood and the Whitestone Creek."

"Yes Sir," replied Hailey. Then as she peeped around at the dwarf, she added, "I just love those little, dwarf horses."

"No such a thing," responded Grimm quickly. "They're Shelties. I'm the only dwarf here."

"Yes Sir," managed Hailey weakly as she noted her sister's laughing.

A sharp kick on the left shin only managed to increase the laughter.

"None of that," said Grimm. "Thus far, you've been perfect ladies. Don't make me rethink that assumption."

"Yes Sir," replied the girls in unison.

After an hour or so, and a good deal of pony coaxing from the dwarf, the Shetlands had the little group approaching the front yard of the Nutt place. The girls stood, noticing their parents in the front yard. Russell was synching the saddle on his horse and Heather was holding a cloth bag full of something.

Before the girls had a chance to call to them, Heather dropped the bag to the grass and grabbed her cheeks with her hands. "Oh my word!" she exclaimed loudly. "The girls are here!"

Then, with tears welling up in her eyes, she ran for the wagon. Russell walked quickly behind her, leading his horse.

"We found your clothes and tools at the stream where you last worked," said Heather. She wiped the tears from her eyes and looked curiously at Grimm.

"What happened?" asked Russell. He stared at the dwarf and added, "Their clothes were torn and soiled. We've spent most of the night in the woods but found not one sign that made sense—a woman's tracks that led from the pool to nowhere, a wolf's tracks that came and went as she did, and not a single sign of the girls leaving the pool at all."

"I have no doubt," answered Grimm. "They've had some trouble with a very bad person--Laphidius Monks be her name."

"Monks?" echoed Russell as he glanced at the dwarf. "I've never heard of her."

"Uhhh," Grimm looked back at the two girls.

"A Witch," said Ashley. "And she put a spell on us that shrunk us up as small as faeries, and that's who helped us."

Heather stepped a bit closer and squinted at the two. "Faeries? A Witch? A spell?" Was all she could muster at first. The look on her face was more than just concern, it was one of disbelief, one of denial, one of shock, one of anger, and one of relief all rolled up into one itching ball. She then finally mustered up, "And helped by? . . . By? . . . By?"

"Faeries," said Grimm weakly, keeping his eyes glued to Russell.

Russell rolled his eyes, stepped around Heather, took hold of the front of the buggy, and then glared at Grimm. "Are you the one who's been giving my girls mushrooms?" he asked angrily.

"No Sir," replied Grimm, "but I could use one or two right now."

"I can prove it," said Hailey. She fished out a small, brown, deerskin pouch from her pocket and then held it up by its drawstrings. "Wow," she added excitedly. "I guess it was also made bigger when Be--"

"When I helped them—me, Bombed Grimm," interrupted the dwarf loudly.

"Well," replied Russell. He released the wagon and

stepped back a bit.

"You stole it," said Ashley, looking at the pouch. "That belongs to Rosebud."

"Borrowed it," corrected Hailey. "I knew we would be in a pickle trying to explain all of this to everyone. Besides, I'm gonna send it back with Grimm."

"What did you say they called it?" asked Ashley as she reached for took hold of the pouch.

"It's not really mine," exclaimed Hailey as she gently tried to pull it back.

"Be careful with that," warned the dwarf. "Keep that stuff in the pouch!"

Ashley quickly let the pouch go causing Hailey's hand to lurch backward, stopping just short of her mother's blouse. When it did, a silvery-blue stream of glittering fog shot from the neck of the bag and struck Heather just under the chin.

"Merciful dragons," groaned Grimm as he covered his face with his left hand and slowly shook his head.

"Well at least it looks pretty," said Heather as she tried to brush the glittering dust from her blouse.

"Get hold of her, Sir" advised Grimm, looking at Russell. He quickly opened the rear door of the buggy and stepped out.

"What's happening?" asked Heather, noting she could hardly keep her balance.

"In the house with her!" exclaimed Grimm as Ashley and Hailey scrambled from the buggy.

Then, with Hailey holding her mother's left arm and Ashley holding her right, they guided her toward the front porch.

Russell, still wide-eyed and speechless, just followed and watched without a word.

Grimm raced up the steps and opened the front door. "Don't turn loose," he warned. "If we lose her, we'll be all day chasin' her down."

"What'll we do? Does this stuff wear off?" asked Ashley as they pulled a now speechless Heather into the living room.

"Eventually," answered Grimm, "but for now, I got

an idea."

* * *

A short while later, Heather sat in her favorite rocking chair by the window with a large garden stone in her lap. Finally, after a good stretch of silence, she asked, "What did they look like?"

"Who, Mummy?" asked Ashley.

"Why . . . the faeries of course—the ones who helped you two."

Hailey smiled and then replied, "Before or after the mushrooms?

Fourth Offering: Doppelganger

The quiet, little city of Oxford, Mississippi had always been a safe place for cyclist Brenda Coons. The warm, August, night air was like a sauna on her face as she coasted along Cleveland Street. About the time she thought she should slow down, she noticed an electric gate opening on the left side of the road. But what she didn't see was the powerful Mustang that roared out onto the lane . . .

"God!" she exclaimed as she gripped the handlebars of her Wildwood Diamondback Hybrid.

Sliding more than slowing, she hardly had the time to scream. With a burnt-orange flash of color and a gut wrenching thump-crunch, she found herself in the air, sailing over a shallow drainage ditch. She never felt the old, oak she hit . . .

* * *

A cool, damp cloth on a warm face would comfort most anyone, but the only thing Brenda could think of as she came around was the screaming pain in her left thigh.

"Try not to move, please," said a voice to her right.

"Sweet Jesus," she groaned weakly as she tried to open her eyes.

Blurry red and yellow flashes from the corner of her right eye was
all she could see.

"You'll be fine, Miss," assured the voice again. "Just be still and let me work."

"I can't see," said Brenda weakly.

"I know," the voice came again. "You've got a bad cut on your forehead and the blood has matted your eyes closed. Your left leg is broken below the knee. I'll need to put a splint on it before we put you on the stretcher. Can you feel your legs?"

"You bet. The left one is killing me."

"I've given you a shot, but it will still hurt a bit when I set it."

The voice sounded familiar—a young man to be sure.

"Try not to move your head," he spoke again as gentle hands cradled her neck. "This is a brace in case your neck is injured."

But then, the gentle hands moved to her left thigh. Brenda screamed, and then all was dark.

*   *   *

The next thing she knew, she was in a bed, a bit firm for her liking, and everything was pleasantly cool. The smell of fresh sheets with a light fragrance of alcohol taunted her.

Slowly opening her eyes to a bright, white ceiling, she quickly reached for her neck. *The brace is gone,* she thought.

She then rolled her head to the right—a small closet and an equally small bathroom.

"Welcome back," spoke a familiar voice to her left.

Brenda slowly turned her head. He was tall, dark-haired, her age, and had the gentlest brown eyes she had ever seen. They seemed to be smiling at her. She quickly tried to check her long, blonde hair, but it seemed useless. It was tied tightly behind her head.

He's about twenty-five. Just a little older than me, she thought.

"How do you feel?" he asked as he walked to the left side of her bed.

"Terrible. I'm aching all over. Ohhh my gosh!" she said as her cell phone rang.

"Don't move. Your phone is right here," said the young man.

"It's Miss Lucy. Tell her I'm fine."

Brenda listened to his voice as he explained to Miss Lucy what happened. When he hung up, she smiled at him and said, "I know you're not the one who helped me, but I've heard your voice before."

"I don't doubt it," quipped the young man. "I have

that effect on all the good-looking girls it seems.

"I'm feeling better already," said Brenda as she tried to sit up.

"No, no, no," responded the young man as Brenda winced and then grabbed her left side.

The young fellow quickly slipped his arms around her shoulders and lowered her back to her pillow. "Just put your pretty, little, blue-eyed, blonde head right back down," he instructed.

"I know that voice," said Brenda through forced smile. "Tell me who you are right now."

"William Grube," replied the young man, smiling back at her. "You can call me Bill."

"My creative writing class at Old Miss," she said just above a whisper. "You are in it."

"Correct," replied Bill. "Looks like your guardian angel went to sleep on you yesterday.

"Yes." Brenda sighed. "But that would be his first time."

"'His' first time?"

"Absolutely. I've been aware of him ever since I was old enough to know I could dream."

"You've actually seen him?" asked Bill.

"Not at first," replied Brenda with a slight smile. "When I was a child, he would talk to me in my dreams. You know, like a parent looking over your shoulder. Then, just before I entered my teens, he rescued me from a booger bear—in a dream of course." Brenda then laughed at Bill's 'oh brother' expression. "Give me a break," she then quipped. "I was only twelve. That's when he told me his name—Dilyn."

Bill raised his eyebrows. "That's Walsh for shadow. See him often?" he added.

"About two or three times a year or so after that. My father said it was just a phase and I would grow out of it."

"And . . ." Bill raised his eyebrows.

"He's still around." She forced another smile.

"This is getting better by the minute," said Bill. "What does he look like?"

"Are you making fun of me?" grumbled Brenda. Her expression clouded up like a tropical rainstorm.

"No-no-no," said Bill quickly. "I would never do that. I just saw the beginning of a great story. Have you ever written about him?"

Brenda slowly shook her head. "Never write about anything I'm living." She then looked back at him and asked, "Did they catch the person who hit me?"

"No, I'm afraid. He came back, but was scared off by the one who called us. The important part here is that he might be a murder suspect and it looks like you're the only witness."

"Someone was killed?" Brenda winced as she pushed herself up against her pillow. "Where did this happen?"

"Where you got hit. There's a cop outside your door right now and he's hardly letting a soul in."

"No way," she said weakly looking toward the door."

"Can we come in?" spoke an older man with a gentle knock on the now-opening door.

Just stepping through the doorway were two, middle-aged gentleman. The dark suits, loosened ties, and hopeful looks on their faces screamed police.

"Ohhh Lord," groaned Brenda, "Men in black already, and I never saw the UFO that hit me."

"I like that," replied the dark-haired one, earning a silent sneer from his slightly overweight partner. "I'm Richard Walsh and this Kojack-looking fellow is my partner, James Kahn. We're detectives from Oxford."

With his hair neatly kempt, shoes polished, and a hint of Aqua Velva, Walsh brought a smile to Brenda's face.

"I'll ask the questions," said the bald-headed one.

"I'd rather you didn't," insisted Brenda. "I need a little levity right now."

"Good," said Inspector Walsh as he pulled up a straight-back chair and sat down by the right side of the bed.

"I really didn't have time to see much, Mr. Walsh," said Brenda. "I heard it was a Mustang and I know it was burnt orange."

"Burnt orange," grumbled Inspector Kahn. "What kind of color is that?"

"Reddish brown," explained Walsh as he winked at Brenda and then added, "He only knows black and white. Are you sure it came out of the Brandon residence?" he added.

"If that's the one with the black iron, rolling gate, across from where I ended up, that's the one. What's this about a murder?" she added as she slowly sat up.

"A lawyer was murdered there," answered Walsh. "Personally, I think this was a mob hit. The problem now is the pro now thinks you saw him and that's not good for you. We're gonna give you a little protection until we get a handle on this hit man."

Brenda rolled her eyes as she plopped back down on her pillow.

"I'll stay with her also," said Bill, smiling at Brenda. "I've got vacation left and besides, I'm cheaper than a nurse."

"Actually," interrupted Walsh, "that wouldn't be such a bad idea. I'll have a man on the outside and William will be on the inside."

"Look," said Inspector Kahn, rubbing his stomach. "It's eleven o'clock. I'm going down to the cafeteria and get something before the twelve o'clock crowd gets there."

"Believe I'll join them," said Bill.

"Good," agreed Walsh, "Take the detective with you and bring me a ham on rye and a cup of Joe." He then turned to Brenda and added, "I'll be right outside the door, sweetie. Do you want anything?"

"No thanks," said Brenda, waving weakly at the Inspector as the the two left.

Brenda slid down on her pillow a bit, pulled up the thin spread, and then shut her eyes. The soft voices in the hallway and the melodious tones from the nurse's desk and elevator soon faded. With the pain in her leg finally subsiding, she drifted off to sleep. A gentle breeze seemed to caress her face, and with it came the scent of rain that always accompanied her imaginary friend. Soon, she could hear her father's old kitchen fan whirring in the little, clapboard house of her childhood on Willow Creek.

* * *

"Change of the guard?" asked a cute, little, brown-eyed blond nurse as she paused in front of Inspector Walsh now sitting outside Brenda's door.

Walsh immediately stood, eying the little, covered tray she was holding.

"Just something for pain," added the nurse as she lifted the cloth to show a hypodermic with safety cap in place.

"Thanks. I'm sure she could use that."

Walsh quickly let the nurse in and then sat back down.

* * *

Once inside, the nurse quickly looked about the room, checked the bathroom, and then walked to the near side of Brenda's bed.

"All too easy," she whispered, noting that Brenda was fast asleep.

Flipping the alcohol swab and safety cap to the floor, she directed the needle toward the little blue vein in Brenda's outstretched arm. Pushing lightly, she made but a dimple in the young girl's skin. Trying again, a bit harder this time, only produced the same results.

Holding the hypo up to check its needle, her chin dropped slightly. "Bent?" she said just above a whisper.

Then, she noticed something moving on the far side of the needle. Lowering the hypodermic, she watched a shadow-like figure starting to obscure the girl's face. As the apparition formed Brenda's shoulders and arms became hidden.

"What the—" started the nurse as she tried to back away.

Failing to be able to do so, she became aware that something was holding her arm, and it wasn't the girl. She was still asleep in the bed.

"Let me go!" the nurse exclaimed, being as quiet as the moment would allow.

Through the covers the shadowy ghost came, but moved not the smallest wrinkle. With eyes as bright as a welder's arc, its hair was as black as tar, and twisted in tufts, which pointed in every direction. Its ears were long and pointed, extending well up into its hair.

The apparition slowly stood, leaned forward, and then looked down upon the cowering nurse. "Though shalt not kill," spoke a low, guttural voice, the sound of which seemed to resonate deep within the nurse's own chest.

"Let me gooo!" screamed the nurse as she twisted free and then ran for the door, which seemed to open by itself.

"What's going on?" asked Walsh as he tried to step inside.

All but bowling him over, the little nurse pushed past him. "There's something in there with the girl!" she exclaimed as she ran down the hallway.

With his hand on his Smith and Wesson nine, the inspector eased into the room. When he was no more than two steps inside, he caught a glimpse of a shadowy figure as it sprung toward the bathroom from the side of Brenda's bed.

"Police," shouted the Inspector. "Stop right there!"

Walsh quickly turned the corner of the little entranceway to the room only to find the bathroom door still closed. Now, with the Smith and Wesson out, he eased the door open and peeped inside—nothing but the strong scent of rain.

"What's happening?" asked Brenda as she rubbed her eyes and tried to sit up.

"You just stay right there, Sweetie, until I get a handle on what the devil is going on." said the Inspector.

"Who are you?" demanded a voice right behind him.

"Geeze!" exclaimed Walsh as he turned to see a security guard. "Never scare a man with a gun in his hand. I'm Inspector Walsh. Someone or something scared the nurse just in here."

"The nurse is at the desk, Inspector," explained the guard. "Someone knocked her out fifteen minutes ago."

Walsh turned to see a redheaded nurse step around the guard and walk to Brenda's bed.

"Where's the blond nurse?" asked Walsh.

"I'm afraid I'm it until four," said the nurse. "There's not a blond on this floor."

"What's going on, Richard?" asked Inspector Kahn as he, the patrolman, and Bill rushed into the room.

Walsh looked at the group, paused, and then asked, "You didn't possibly see a gorgeous, little blond on your way up here did you? She could possibly be dressed like a nurse."

"Afraid not," answered Kahn as the patrolman and Bill also shook their heads.

"What's happening Mr. Walsh?" asked Brenda again. "You've got your gun out."

Return his weapon to his holster, Inspector Walsh replied, "We just had another visit from your UFO friend. She bopped the nurse here on the head, got past me dressed as a nurse, and then almost got at you, but something scared her off."

"Her?" asked Kahn.

"Yes, James, our hit man is a hit woman—all blond and beautiful."

Walsh rolled his eyes, but kept his hand on it as he peeped into the bathroom again.

"What are you doing?" asked Kahn.

"Chasing my tail, I think," answered Walsh as he glanced at Brenda.

Kahn then slowly shook his head and asked, "Do you mind putting that in English?"

"All right," groaned Walsh as he faced the group. "The fake nurse went in here to give Brenda a shot. Shortly after she got in, I heard a scream. When I opened the door, the nurse came by me like Satan himself was after her. She said something was in here with Brenda. When I stepped in here, I got a glimpse of a shadowy form leaping from beside the bed toward the bathroom."

Walsh then paused, looking at Brenda.

"Well," snapped Kahn. "The bathroom's only three steps away. Did it or did it not go in?"

Walsh raised his eyebrows, scratched the back of his head, and then replied, "If I answer that, it's gonna sound like I just fell off the wagon."

"I'll chance it," responded Kahn.

The Inspector rolled his eyes and continued, "All right, but here comes the 'wagon' part. When I stepped around the corner of the bed where you're standing, I found the bathroom door closed."

"Closed?" queried Kahn.

"Yep."

A slight grin began to form on Kahn's face as he asked, "What happened to this 'shadow' thing?"

"Not a clue. No one was inside the bathroom."

Kahn paused a minute noting Brenda as she looked at Bill's slack-jawed expression. "You two know something about this, don't you?" he then asked, as he looked straight at Brenda. "Were you awake during all of this?"

Brenda slunk down on her pillow but didn't indicate yes or no.

"Well, were you," demanded Inspector Kahn as he stepped to the foot of her bed.

"No. I didn't see it this time," admitted Brenda.

"Please explain 'not this time' if you will," asked Kahn.

"Her doppelganger," guessed Bill.

"Kahn then looked directly at Walsh and said, "I'm not writing this report, Richard. We have a drop dead gorgeous hit woman, shadows that walk through doors, and now this doppelganger thing, and I don't even know what that is."

"It's a ghost of a living person--one that watches over you," explained Brenda.

Kahn lowered his head as if looking over a pair of invisible glasses and then replied, "Do you expect me to believe that Sci-Fi, mumbo-jumbo crap?"

"Believe what you will," replied Brenda quickly. "That word means 'Double Walker' in German. As far back as the third century, the English believed that to mean your embodied conscious, or if you will, your guardian angel."

Kahn then turned to see a middle-aged fellow step into the room. He had graying temples, and was dressed in a doctor's white coat.

Walsh quickly looked at his ID badge. "How is she, Dr. Rhea?" he asked, glancing quickly at the nurse.

"He's real, Inspector," she replied through a slight grin.

The doctor then walked to the left side of the bed, put his left hand on her wrist, and then paused. "You're a very lucky, young lady, Miss Coons," he finally said. "The cut on your head looks much worse than it really is. You have three, slightly cracked ribs. The nurse is going to fit you in a support vest. Wear it as much as possible. Your left leg has a clean break. Your EMT did a good job in setting and immobilizing it. That lessened the surrounding tissue damage dramatically." He then smiled at her and added, "I think you'll be getting out of here about six this afternoon. How does that suit you?"

"Much quicker than I expected," answered Brenda with a bit of a smile. "That'll give me a little time to call my boss and tell him he'll have to do without a frame girl for a while."

Walsh then turned to Kahn and said, "I'm staying with the girl. If Blondie gets past me one more time, I'll eat my hat. Take the Ford and check the crime scene. I'll later go to Miss Coon's home with the patrolman.

* * *

Later that afternoon, Brenda's wheelchair came rolling in the door with William Grube at the handles.

Brenda struggled to the mirror, eying her new dress. "This tent thing makes me look absolutely weird," she complained.

"Tan looks good on you," said Walsh. He then pushed the wheelchair closely behind her and added. "By the way, where do you live?"

"Do you know where the old Faulkner place is on Buchanan Road?"

"I'll say. He's my favorite actor."

"Author," whispered Bill.

Brenda laughed and then said, "I live just three miles past it on a winding, little street called Cleveland. It's a quaint, old cottage. My Aunt Jean had it fixed up just before she passed. Her maid and life-time friend still lives there with me."

* * *

Thirty minutes later, put Bill and Brenda cruising down a little winding road near the outskirts of Oxford with a police escort.

"Right here," said Brenda as she pointed at a winding drive, framed by two, huge magnolias on both sides.

"Wow," said Bill softly, noting the little, redwood cottage a bit beyond the flowering trees. "That place looks like it should be on a Sardis Lake instead of hiding under those huge white oaks. Who mows your grass? This yard is huge."

Laughing silently, Brenda replied, "You, hopefully."

"I had to ask," said Bill just above a whisper as he eased the white, Silverado close to the front porch.

The squad car pulled up alongside with Walsh being the first one out. "Check the back," he said to the officer and then walked around to the pickup. "Give me the keys to the house," he said to Brenda, "I want to have a look inside before you two go in."

As Bill retrieved the wheelchair from the truck bed, the Inspector eased the front door open and then slipped inside.

"Get back!" came a shout from the cabin as Walsh quickly backed from the doorway and onto the wrap-around front porch. With his hands raised up in front of him, he eyed the straw end of the old, worn out broom she was holding up between them.

"Ohhh, my God, I forgot to remind him about Mrs. Lucy," exclaimed Brenda as she quickly sat down in the wheelchair. "It's all right Mrs. Lucy," added Brenda loudly while encouraging Bill to get her closer to the porch.

"She hit me," said Walsh, trying desperately to hold back a smile. The wave in his black hair was now dangling down in front of his face.

"I'll do mor'n dat," said the tight-lipped little black lady as she continued to back the Inspector closer to the steps. "You scared me," she added, shaking the broom. "Don't you ever do dat again."

"No ma'am," replied Walsh, glancing again at Brenda.

"Miss Brenda, you all right?" asked Miss Lucy, eying the wheel chair and Bill. "Who is dat boy behind de chair?"

"He's a friend and a classmate, Miss Lucy. I'm afraid we're in a bit of a pickle right now."

"You best hope dey sweet pickles," said Miss Lucy. Squinting back at Walsh, she shook the broom as she added, "Stop dat grinnin'."

"Calm down, Miss Lucy," said Brenda as Bill rolled her to the steps. "They'll be staying with us for at least tonight."

"Child," started the heavy-set lady weakly, "what has you got yo'self into now? If it ain't writin' 'bout spooks, murders, and haints, you is seein' 'em. I been worried stiff since you didn't come in last night. Called everybody I know, an' never fount nobody knowin' nothin' 'bout no Brenda Coons."

I'm sorry, Miss Lucy," said Brenda as Bill and the Inspector lifted her and the wheelchair onto the front porch. "I was all but run over by some lunatic just this side of the old Faulkner home. I didn't really come to myself until late this morning."

"Well," said Miss Lucy as she held the screen door open, "you all get in here where it's cool. I got two chickens in the fridge I can fry 'em up if you all is hungry."

"That would be like heaven, Miss Lucy, assured Brenda.

"Sounds good to me," agreed Walsh. "I'll just be in the back trying to blend in. The patrolman will be in the front with the car. If anyone comes calling, they'll see the car first, but hopefully not me."

Miss Lucy immediately looked at Brenda. "What do he mean by 'anyone'," she asked. Her eyebrows rose as though leery of her answer.

"They think girl who hit me killed someone. I saw her car come out from where the victim lived."

"She tried to kill her this morning at the Baptist Hospital," added Walsh. "To ignore a second attempt would be foolish."

Miss Lucy stood there with her eyes glued to the Inspector. "Sweet baby Jesus," she finally got out weakly. "If dis child's haint don't get me, some maniac gonna try? What next?"

"Do you have a dog?" asked the patrolman. "I thought I saw one run around to the back when we drove up."

"German Shepherd," answered Miss Lucy. "But I don't know what we have now. When Miss Jean was around, you wouldn't be able to get out o' dem cars at all. But when Miss Brenda come, ole Snookie got as shy as a witch's cat. Won't even come in de house no more. When Miss Brenda come close, she jus' ducks her head, tucks her tail 'tween her legs, and slips out o' sight. If'n she ever makes you nervous, jus' call her name."

* * *

Later, as afternoon slipped away and the shades of evening began to darken, Miss Lucy sat by one of the windows in her old rocker, pondering over her crochet piece. Bill sat on the couch with Inspector Walsh, staring at the cold logs in the fireplace. Although the leftover plate of Miss Lucy's fried chicken was heavy on his mind, he remained much too bashful to ask for another piece.

Brenda hobbled over on wooden crutches and then sat down beside Bill. "Penny for your thoughts," she said through a warm smile.

"Lots of things," quipped Bill. "The police outside and inside waiting for who knows what, the doppelganger you explained to us earlier, that shadow thing the Inspector chased in the bathroom back at the hospital, and--"

"Mr. Man," interrupted Miss Lucy as she plopped her crochet piece down in her lap, "you leave dat haint be. I can't count stitches and loops with such talk."

"All right, Miss Lucy," said Brenda through a silent chuckle. "We'll--"

Her comment was cut short by a loud thrum-crunch coming from the front yard.

Miss Lucy froze, gripping her needlework as Bill spun around, turned off the pole lamp next to the couch, and then peeped through the window curtains.

"The patrol car just hit the oak on the north-west side of the house," replied Bill. Then, jumping from the couch, he added, "The patrolman is slumped over the wheel. I'll go and check. Everyone just keep calm and stay right here."

"Sweet baby Jesus!" exclaimed Miss Lucy. As her needlework fell to the carpet beside the rocker, she watched the Inspector ease out of the front door and onto the front porch. She then scrambled from the chair and grabbed Brenda's left arm. "Let's go to my room, baby. It's got a dead bolt."

"Is there a gun in the house?" asked Bill as he followed the two from the living room.

Miss Lucy shook her head and replied, "Most dangerous thing in dis house is my broom, and dis ain't broom time."

Lord help us, thought Bill as he ducked in the kitchen and then spotted a big butcher knife on the counter.

Just as he picked it up, he heard a crash in the living room and just knew the front door was gone. Clutching the knife by its point, he quickly stepped into the hallway and threw the weapon toward the two silhouettes in the doorway.

"Damn!" exclaimed a female voice as the sharp hiss of a silencer punctuated her complaint.

The intense pain in Bill's left side told him they didn't exactly miss. Clutching his side, he spun around and dove back into the kitchen as the silencer spoke again. Hearing the bullet shatter the door molding just behind his head, he collided with the counter and quickly opened the first drawer he came to.

Towels, he thought as he turned and then slid down the front of the counter to the floor. Slowly looking up, he saw the two figures now standing in the doorway staring right at him.

"I got the hero," spoke a female voice. "You go and take care of the girl and her maid."

The second gunman quickly headed toward the back. Bill closed his eyes, listened to the gunman beat on

Miss Lucy's door, and then braced for what was coming.

"Though shalt not kill," spoke a deep, guttural voice from the hallway.

Bill looked up just in time to see the gun moll jerked from the floor and fly through the ceiling like smoke through a screen door.

* * *

"What'll we do, Miss Lucy?" whispered Brenda as the two quickly scooted under the double bed.

"Quiet, child. I'm thinkin'"

Then, with one powerful kick, the molding shattered and the bedroom door flew open.

"I know you're in here," spoke what sounded like a man.

Miss Lucy watched as a pair of black wingtip shoes stepped in the bedroom. "Don't shoot, mister," she said as she placed a firm hand on Brenda's mouth.

"Come out from under there," grumbled the man.

Miss Lucy slowly struggled from under the bed. But as she stood up, a strange calmness came over her like the first warm water of a shower. Fear, somehow, completely left her as she eyed the gunman.

"Why are you smiling?" asked the gunman.

"Don't rightly know, Sir," said Miss Lucy. "I jus' feel different somehow."

Then, as the gunman raised his automatic, the form of the black lady changed. Now, standing where she was, was a thin, gray-haired, white lady. Her dim, blue eyes filled with tears as she looked back at the gunman. "Mother?" said the gunman weakly. In disbelief, he lowered his weapon.

"I have just begged for a chance to help you, Teddy. Don't waste it. Put that gun down and go and help the one you hit outside."

But, before the gunman could answer, the image in front of him then changed again.

"Do I get you now?" spoke a seven-foot shadowy figure. With blinding, white eyes as it stood there looking down on him.

Now, still under the bed, Brenda could see little

save Miss Lucy's feet. The pistol falling to the floor and the sound of someone running down the hall was just too much for her. All but moving the bed itself, she pushed out beside her friend. As she struggled to stand, she could see the back of the strange voice who had last spoken. The shadowy figure was standing between Miss Lucy and the doorway.

Miss Lucy quickly grabbed Brenda's right hand and pulled her to her feet. "Stand with me, baby, and don't you move a muscle," she whispered. "I'm so scared I could turn ta stone."

Brenda slowly looked from Miss Lucy and to the shadowy figure. Black, feathered, wings all but covered its entire back. The folded corners of which were pointed and almost touched the nine-foot ceiling of the old home. Miss Lucy squeezed Brenda's hand as he turned. Then, through eyes that looked like light reflected off chrome, he looked down at the two cowering in front of him.

"Please, Mr. Dilyn Sir," pleaded Miss Lucy. "I'll never call you a haint again if you'll jus' deliver us from dis mess we in."

The shocking figure then slowly pointed to a locket Miss Lucy always wore around her neck. "Remember the mustard seed, Lucy Brown, and hold to that truth," spoke the angel as he slowly spread his wings. Then, with one, powerful bound, the Angel flew from the floor, passing through the ceiling as if it wasn't there.

"Everything all right here?" asked Walsh as he peeped through the door.

The Inspector stared, anticipating an answer, but all he got from the two ladies was a silent return of his stare.

"Strangest thing happened to me just a minute ago," he continued. "When I went to check the officer in the patrol car, a young woman almost fell on me. She fell right out of the tree the car hit and landed right on the hood. Her gun was lying right there beside her. Then, as I was reviving the officer inside the car, a strange man, dressed in black just like the young lady, came running out the front door. He fell to his knees, and gave up right there in front of me. Would you believe he was crying?"

"How is Bill?" asked Brenda.

"Caught one through the left side," said the Inspector. "I've got an ambulance on the way. They need to tend to him and check those outside. Now tell me, what the devil has just happened."

"Ohhh my God!" exclaimed Brenda as she past the Inspector and on down the hall.

Bill was holding his side, leaning against the kitchen doorway, and smiling.

"No devil," answered Miss Lucy as she and the Inspector walked to join Bill and Brenda. "He's a real out-uh-dis-world person," she added, looking at the Inspector. "Ain't no regular angel neither." She then looked right at Brenda and added, "He be guardin' you for somethin'. If dat's so, den I wan'na be 'round when the whatever happens?"

"Happens?" asked Brenda, looking at Bill quietly laughing.

"I like this story," said Bill. He hugged Brenda, kissed her forehead, and then added, "I believe I'll stick around to see how it ends."

"Happily every after?" said Brenda as she looked up into his eyes.

Bending down for a kiss was painful for Bill, but he made the trip nonetheless.

Fifth Offering: Quest for the Dragon's Scale

Gadritch Brownthum brushed his long, brown hair from his face as he nervously watched the limp directional wind flag on the bow of his gondola. Appearing to be sixty or so, the heavyset dwarf looked down at Broderick Cliffspring from the helm's seat and said, "A little more air if you please Mr. Dwarf. We don't want to settle too quickly."

Sweat glistened in Broderick Cliffspring's red beard as the dwarf pumped a four-foot, makeshift bellows attached to a wood-burning stove. His blue eyes glistened as he watched another dwarf who was now leaning over the side.

"Fifty feet and holdin'," shouted Boegus Gladling. As the black-bearded dwarf rose up from the side of the willow-wicker gondola, he grumbled, "Dwarves should be in tha mines, Captain Dwarf, not floatin' around up here with tha pigeons."

The trim-looking, middle-aged dwarf then picked up a grappling pole and looked back at Gadritch in the helm's seat.

"Off the bellows and find us a clearing," said Gadritch. "We've lost the wind altogether. Get the grapplin' poles and try to keep us out of tha trees as we go down. If we wreck this craft we'll have a long walk back to Leachenwood."

"Over there," said Broderick loudly, pointing directly ahead of them. "If we can just pull ourselves around this here next big oak, we'll have a clear spot on tha far side."

Boegus winced as the as the hull of the boat-shaped, willow woven gondola scratched its way through the top of the old oak.

"Just a little more," encouraged Gadritch as he leaned from the helm's seat to peer over the side.

"Now!" shouted Broderick, shoving one of the tree's huge limbs away from the stern.

As the limb bounced off the bottom of the gondola, Gadritch nervously tugged on a black rope hanging from the inside of the fig-shaped, blue balloon. Hot air escaped from the top vent as it opened, allowing the craft to settle slowly between the surrounding trees.

"Over the side with a tether rope, Boegus. Quickly now!" ordered Gadritch. "Tie us down to somethin' solid."

Immediately dropping his grappling pole, the black-headed dwarf immediately threw the stern tether rope over the side and slid quietly to the ground. Gadritch watched nervously as the boat-shaped gondola slid softly through the smaller limbs, and settled closer to the ground.

"Over the side, you old, red-bearded spider," shouted Boegus as he watched Broderick inch his way down the bow tether line.

Gadritch shut off the burner, jumped from the helm's seat, and then leaned over the side. "How close are we to where the 'Watcher' is supposed to be," he all but whispered.

Boegus immediately froze, looking at the captain of the dwarves.

Broderick only smiled as he finished tying off the gondola to a large stone. "The whole of Lake Oxbow and the woods between it and the town of Cutoff," he finally answered as he watched Gadritch climb down the ship's rope ladder.

Just as soon as the old dwarf's foot touched the ground, Gadritch looked to him and said, "We'll keep tha burner warm all night. If we don't, the balloon will collapse, and with so little room in these here trees we'll have a fine time getting' it back up." He then squinted at the Captain of the dwarves and added, "And just what do we have to do once we find this wizard's lizard?"

"I'd like to know that, myself," said Boegus. Then, as he stepped a bit closer to Broderick, the dwarf added,

"All's we know now is we have a contest betwixt two captains—you and Feathersmore of the Dragon's Oak elves. Ya mind explainin' that for us?"

"We'll cook a little somethin' before dark sets in," said Broderick through a half-smile. "I'll lay it all out for you two in the mornin' while we have breakfast. I don't think the elves have beat us here. We still have a little time on them and if the wind is in our favor tomorrow, we'll beat 'em across the Oxbow as well. On horses they are, and they may have ta go 'round the lake."

"Very well," grumbled Gadritch. "But if I'm not pleased with it, Boegus and me will drop you off and ride the next wind north."

"Agreed then," said Broderick as he began picking up pieces of wood for the cook fire.

* * *

The first light of the next day crept in as quiet as a mouse's sneeze. Boegus, the only one of the three close to being awake, struggled as he wrestled a pinecone from under his blanket. Now, with his stubby fingers imbedded in his beard, he searched for the illusive field mouse that had been pestering him most of the night. Failing once again to find the little critter, he slid his right arm from under the woolen blanket, grabbed another piece of firewood, and tossed it in the coals.

"Merciful dragons!" exclaimed Broderick as a mound of quilts on the far side of the campfire literally became alive with motion. The bulbous-nosed dwarf quickly sat up, rubbed his eyes, and then glared at the mound of blankets that covered Boegus. "Watch em' embers!" he grumbled. "They still have life in 'em."

"The gnomish lad's lying," said Boegus as he pushed the blankets from him and then slowly sat up. "The elves are probably laughing at us this very minute. Even if we do find the 'Watcher', who's gonna be fool enough to take one of his scales?"

"How'd you know that?" snapped Boegus as he struggled to his feet.

"We both heard you," replied Gadritch as he slowly struggled from beneath his covers as well. "That beast's been chasin' you in your dreams all night long."

"He's not as bad as he looks," mumbled Broderick, "But I just can't get past how he looks." He then looked at Gadritch and added, "We'll find out where the lad lives. The old Wizard Basil has charged the beast with the lad's safe-keepin'. So the dragon will be close there somewheres."

"Soooo," quipped Boegus as he looked at Broderick. "If we actually survive the getting' of the dragon's scale, what's in it for us?"

"The sword of Kebron," replied Broderick. "It's been in Feathersmore's family for years."

"And if we lose?" asked Gadritch.

Broderick looked out into the woods and then weakly said, "The axe of Cromlin."

"That's your grandfather's," said Gadritch.

"The same," mumbled Broderick, "but I don't intend to lose it."

"Then . . . this, formidable creature actually exists," said Boegus weakly.

"He does," answered Broderick. "The gnome, Long Bob, told me himself. He holds a seat on the Board of Elders at the gnomish village of Cutoff. Seems the lad, Yenwolk, got himself in trouble and the dragon had to step in or risk the old wizard's wrath if the lad got hurt. Choosin' the former, he was seen by at least four gnomes."

"Are we eatin' in the gondola this morning?" asked Boegus.

"We might better," answered Gadritch. "Early this mornin' I could have sworn I heard riders pass in the night just west of us. That bein' the case, we might have lost our lead."

"Riders!" exclaimed Broderick. As he and the others scrambled to collect their belongings, he mumbled, "The elves should be afoot."

"Not to worry," assured Gadritch. "They have to go 'round the bend of the lake. We'll go straight across and then pick up the Whitestone Trail on the southern side. Then, it shouldn't be that far before we get to Cutoff. It's quite near the lake's southern shore."

"Done, then," agreed Broderick. "I'll fire up the

furnace while Boegus loads us some more wood. We'll get that willow-wicker ship thing of yours up in the air in no time."

Now, with Broderick on the five-foot bellows, the logs glistened cherry-red as Gadritch kept an eye on how much extra wood Broderick threw into the gondola.

With the craft straining on the ropes, Boegus threw the last handful of wood into the gondola's deck, released the tethers, and then ran for the rope ladder. Barely making it, the nimble dwarf scurried up and onto the deck. With hot air pouring from the top vents of the stove, the craft lifted quickly from the ground.

"Grab the grapplin' poles and keep us off em' trees," ordered Gadritch. "We've got a good southerly wind and should see Oxbow in no time." He turned to Boegus and said, "Put out the jibs. We want to be keepin' her nose in the right direction."

Boegus scurried to the front of the vessel, looped the safety rope around his waist, and then edged out onto the nose of the gondola. Pulling at a rope attached to the bow, two triangular sails unfurled from the short, horizontal mast protruding from the nose of the ship. The bow of the gondola slowly corrected itself, pointing in the direction the craft was moving--straight south toward the lake.

"There it is!" exclaimed Broderick as the gondola rose well above the trees. But then, Broderick remained strangely quiet, with his eyes transfixed on something else in the distance.

Noting that the dwarf captain had obviously spotted something, Gadritch slipped from the helm's seat, eased around the furnace, and joined him. "See somethin'?" he asked.

"Indeed," answered Broderick. he quickly pointed toward the Oxbow Lake. "There's a two-masted ship moving away from the banks. It doesn't have a single sail to tha masts, yet it's making an impressive wake." Broderick looked at Gadritch and added, "How could that be? Are the elves using magic? That's cheatin' that is!"

Gadritch then quickly turned to Boegus and said, "Get into that helm's seat and make sure we hold due south."

"I can't operate this thing," complained Boegus as he climbed into the tall seat.

"How hard could it be with only three ropes?" shouted Gadritch. "Pull the green one on the right and it'll open the left vent a bit. That'll push us gently to the right. Pull the red one on the left and it'll open the vent on the right and we'll go left. But whatever you do, don't touch the black one. It opens the top vent and we'll sink like a rock."

Boegus rolled his eyes, looking at the colored ropes hanging in front of the seat. "Right one attached to the left vent and we go right, but left one hooked to the right one and we go left and..." Boegus rolled his eyes, looking at the black rope. He then pulled his hands away from the rope's wooden handles altogether.

Gadritch then looked back at what Broderick was still puzzling over. "Well, that is a riddle," he quipped.

"Certainly some kind of ship. No sail, but it's still moving fast enough to give us trouble."

"You're the machinist here," said Broderick. "You've made things of black iron, oak wood, and the elfin, white metal. Now tell me just what kind of vessel moves without wind or paddle."

"An elfin one," answered Gadritch. He pointed out the flag atop the first mast.

"A white unicorn on a field of dark blue," said Broderick weakly. "It's Feathersmore all right. He's cheating again."

"He's spelled the whole darned ship," shouted Boegus as he all but stood in the helm's seat.

"Calm down, Boegus, and pull on that red rope just a little bit. You're letting us drift too far to the right."

Little by little, a smile worked its way beneath Gadritch's big, bulbous nose as they closed the distance between them and the ship. "I see it," he replied just above a whisper. "They have a chimney! They're burnin' oak wood an' boilin' water. Steam's pushin' that thing it is!"

"Steam?" quizzed Broderick.

"Certainly. See those wheels turnin' on each side of the ship? There's at least a dozen paddles spinnin' on an axle and it's bein' turned by steam some kind o' way."

"I don't get it," complained Broderick. "I still think it's spelled."

"No, no, no," corrected Gadritch. "It's like you breathin', in and out. The steam off the boilin' water is your breath in. When the machine breathes that steam out, it pushes on a plunger and lever system that turns the axle and spins them paddles."

"Well it's spinnin' pretty good," said Boegus. "Plus, they've just dropped a sail to boot and we've all but stopped gainin' on them."

"Spotted us they have!" exclaimed Gadritch. He spun around, trotted around the furnace, and then ordered, "Get down, Boegus. This simply won't do."

Now, with the elfin vessel taking a more easterly course on the crescent-shaped lake, Gadritch steered straight south.

"I believe we got 'em!" shouted Gadritch. "We'll cut across them woods up there in the middle of the lake's curve. I believe we'll beat 'em to the southern banks. Then, they'll be afoot in the forests between the lake and Cutoff. Now, one of you get to the bow of this thing and help me spot the Whitestone Road when we make the southern banks."

Boegus eased passed the helm's seat, slowed, and then looked up at Gadritch. "But are not those woods south of the Oxbow Lake where the dragon stays?"

Gadritch quickly looked at Broderick, who was now slowly shaking his head in disapproval.

"Maybe," admitted the dwarf captain, "But then again, maybe not. I 'spect the old wizard will have him a bit closer to the lad. He, his mother, and some friends saw him at a place called Sugar Creek Springs. That's a bit south of the Cutoff and quite near his own home I suppose. The old Wizard's son, Benjamin, told me that Yenwolk actually talked to the creature in those woods just behind his home."

"Talked!" exclaimed Gadritch. "How is it that he'll talk to gnomes and not to dwarves anyways?"

Boegus looked disgustedly at Broderick and then added, "Do you blame him? It once was that every time any kind of dragon flew over Leachenwood's entrance one of Broderick's hardheads would turn loose one of those big swing-bows at him. It took the old Wizard Basil, himself, to threaten to seal the entrance of the caverns to get 'um ta quit."

"Ohhh," grumbled Broderick. "That's in the past. The wizards and me got an agreement. Now, Benjamin and I are just like . . ." The dwarf captain tried to cross his stubby fingers on his right hand. In failing to do so, he said, "We're real close anyways."

"Hope so," mumbled Boegus. "Dragons are dragons, and they have long memories." Boegus then looked to the port side of the vessel and exclaimed, "We got 'em! We got 'em! We're over the Oxbow again and the elves are just breakin' 'round the point."

"Just what I expected," said Gadritch as he stood from his helm's seat. "Now get to the bow. We'll be over the Cutoff woods before you know it, and be looking for that wizard's beast too. Bright yellow and green should stand out down there like a peach on a plum tree."

"He won't even see us comin" added Broderick. "Dragons don't have enemies so they hardly ever feel the need to look up."

Gadritch slowly closed the damper on the stove allowing his craft to settle closer to the tops of the trees. "Lay off the bellows, Broderick," he whispered. "All that huffin' and puffin' is sure to attract tha lizard's attention."

"We're not that far from the Cutoff Road," whispered Broderick as he joined Boegus on the bow. "I can see smoke from the village just off the starboard bow. Sugar creek should be dead ahead."

The huge, blue dirigible drifted over the Cutoff road as quiet as an owl's wings. What few gnomes they noticed never bothered to look up. Gadritch chuckled from the helm's seat, completely amused at the accomplishment. Then, as the breeze took them back into the woods south of the road, it soon became quite obvious that dwarves hardly look up either.

“What the devil is that?” exclaimed Gadritch as the gondola shook violently. The old dwarf struggled to keep from being thrown from the helm’s seat.

The lurch was so violent it sent Broderick and Boegus tumbling to the deck. Then, as the vessel lurched again, a noise came more sickening than any stomachache—the sound of ripping canvass.

“It’s like we hit somethin’,” said Boegus, but we’re a good fifty feet above the tallest tree.

“On the bellows, Boegus!” shouted Gadritch. Then, as he opened the dampers as wide as possible, he looked up into the fig-shaped balloon. “We got a huge, six-foot hole right at the top vent! Throw some wood in this thing, Broderick. If we don’t get the heat up in a hurry, we’re gonna drop like ship’s anchor.”

“But . . . but, Broderick’s not here,” said Boegus weakly as he rushed to look down from the port side of the vessel. “We need to put down right now and look for em’!” he shouted as he searched down into the forest.

“Ha!” exclaimed Gadritch loudly. “That’s exactly what we’re doin’. Now pump that bellows or we’ll crack ‘er up entirely.”

* * *

As Boegus frantically pumped the billows of their ‘sinking’ ship, Broderick found himself out of the gondola and clinging to one of the top limbs of a huge white oak. . .

“A fine mess I’m in,” he grumbled as he dangled beneath the huge limb.

Having a bit of trouble maintaining his hold on the tree, he looked toward the body of the old oak. It was larger than the waist of three men.

“Just wonderful,” he mumbled, “I’ll never get a grip around that. Now, just how do I work this out without breakin’ bones?”

“Not with a crossbow,” spoke someone from the ground directly below him.

From the sound of the deep, guttural tone, the dwarf captain knew it was something other than gnomish. With his eyes all but shut, Broderick tried to maintain his grip on the limb. Finally, realizing his hopeless situation, he worked up the nerve to look down.

“Valerie please take me now,” he said weakly as he looked at the creature lying in the leaves below him. His forehands were three times that of any man’s hands, and his length, tail and all, had to be over forty feet at the least.

Noticing the dragon’s bright, yellow eyes, the dwarf looked away, closed his eyes, and then pushed his forehead against the limb he was desperately clinging to.

“Praying to the old oak will not help you there, Master Dwarf,” spoke the voice again. “There are no big limbs between you and I. Just turn loose of the oak. I will catch you.”

Hearing no anger in the beast’s voice, the dwarf looked down once again. Then, trying to ignore the huge, black claws of the creature, Broderick tried to speak, but his mouth was so dry he could hardly make a good start.

“You have me at a disadvantage, Sir,” he finally got out. “If I am to die here, I would at least like to know your name.”

“I know your name,” responded the dragon. “I heard it shouted from that thing you were last in. The Wizard Benjamin has spoken of you in a favorable way. Sooo . . .” The dragon slowly pushed himself up on his haunches, looked up, and then continued, “The only thing that needs be done now is to change your opinion of me.”

“You will not harm me?” asked the dwarf.

The dragon sighed heavily as he looked away from the dwarf and into the dark of the woods. Then, he finally said, “You will fall into my hands eventually, Master Dwarf. It will mean much more to me if you do it on faith than have it happen after your strength fails. After all, if I had wanted you dead, I would have caught you on the way to the tree you are now gripping.”

Broderick slowly shook his head. “I see your point, Sir. Are you ready?”

“More than you, obviously,” responded the dragon impatiently.

The dwarf then closed his eyes, took as deep a breath as possible, and then released his grip on the limb. The wind whistled by his ears. Leaves, acorns, and small limbs stung his neck and back as he fell. But when he hit, it was as if he fell into his own goose-down mattress.

"You can open your eyes now," spoke the dragon as he gazed amused at the being now cupped in his hands.

The dwarf slowly peeped up through his fingers at the one holding him. Following the yellow scales up the underside of the beast's chin, his eyes just could not get past the creature's teeth. They were meshed together like the veins of a feather. The dragon then lowered his forehands to the grass and sat the dwarf in front of him.

"Thank you, Sir," said Broderick as he struggled to his feet. "I owe you. If it weren't for you, this might have been the end of me."

"You are a friend of Benjamin. You can repay me by making a friend of the boy Yenwolk. I heard you speak of him as I followed above your craft."

"Tell me," said the dwarf. "Do your scales ever itch?"

The dragon pushed himself up a bit straighter, looked down at the dwarf, and then said, "What sort of a question is that? Do your fingernails ever itch?"

"Well, no, not really," answered Broderick. He then asked just above a whisper, "Then, it would probably hurt to pull one off for someone wouldn't it?"

"It wouldn't feel good," replied the dragon as he narrowed his eyes at the dwarf. "Just what are you up to? A group of elves are also a bit south of here and in equally as big a hurry in the same direction your craft was taking."

"We . . . Uh . . . are looking for the one who watches the boy, Yenwolk."

"You seek the Wizard Benjamin's dragon," replied the creature. "You seek Pandahar."

"Yes. The one who watches the young gnome."

"And just what part does this scale play?" asked the dragon suspiciously.

The dwarf marveled at the intelligence of the creature sitting before him, looked into the woods, and then sighed heavily. "Proof we saw him," he finally got out.

The huge creature slowly shook his head, raised

himself from the ground, and then backed up a bit. "I will not play your game," he added as he stretched his wings out and shook them. "Seek the boy who is watched. He has your proof, but it should cost you. He got it from me."

Then, in a flurry of leaves and pine needles, the great-winged, forest dragon leapt into the air. The canopy hardly moved as the huge creature slipped between the trees to disappear above their limbs.

Broderick sat down hard on the leaves and rubbed his face briskly. "Merciful dragons," he said through a heavy sigh. "I thought I was a goner," he added weakly. He slowly looked back up to where he last saw the dragon. "So. . .that is what the gnomes call 'The Pan'. I have made a valuable friend indeed."

The snickering in the scrub just south of him then quickly made Broderick realize he still wasn't alone.

"Boegus, you black-bearded hobbit!" shouted Broderick. "Is the vessel still in one piece?" he grumbled.

Boegus slowly stood from within the short bushes. "Yes, but it's jus' like you--down, in shock, and too weak to stand," laughed the dwarf as he stepped from the tangles .

"Very funny," grumbled Broderick as he struggled to his feet. "What did we hit?"

"Not sure, but whatever it was will keep Gadritch sewing for a while. He said he'd repair the thing while we go to the village and find that boy."

"Good," replied Broderick. Then, as he looked toward the south-east, he added, "We're a little sough of the Cutoff Road and probably real close to his house." He then stepped a bit closer to Boegus and said through a little grin, "The 'Watcher' saved my bacon. He also told me that young Yen has one of his scales. Feathersmore surely can't know this. But, if he does, the race is truly on. We need to get to the road and seek help from the first gnome we come across. That's the only way I know to find where the lad lives."

* * *

It wasn't long until it became obvious that Broderick was right. As they drew near the rear of a little cabin, he waved at a young girl working in her garden.

"Good day to you, my Lady," he called.

She paused, wiped the sweat from her brow, and leaned on her hoe. Brushing her long, brown hair from her forehead, she held the smile and replied, "I thought the dwarf village was to the north."

Boegus grinned. "Ahhh yes, Leachenwood," he quipped. "It is, but we took a shortcut. Could you tell us where the Stonesmith cabin is? We're looking for the lad, Yenwolk."

"Right there," she answered, pointing to a cabin and barn not more than a hundred yards east of them. "I'm Belinda Pragen. The Stonesmiths are our best friends. They've had lots of visitors this year. I've seen elves there as well. There's even a group of them there now. I noticed them ride across the road from the lake just minutes before you came up."

"Elves!" exclaimed Boegus.

"Ride?" asked Broderick. "How in this mother's son did they come by horses?"

Boegus shrugged his shoulders. "They're the only somebody's who can summon mounts up from the forest with but a whistle."

"Thank you for your time," said Broderick as he quickly nodded to Belinda, turned to Boegus, and then said, "We must go. It may be that they don't know what the young gnome holds. Besides, we have permission to the scale by the Pan himself."

As they walked briskly through the garden between the two homes, Boegus pointed toward the cabin. "There they are," he said just above a whisper. "I can see a couple of their horses tied on the far side of the house."

"Magic," grumbled Broderick. "Feathersmore cheated. Somehow, I know they all cheated."

"Did you say they couldn't use magic?" asked Boegus, watching his friend's expression closely.

"Not sure," grumbled Broderick as they stepped from the garden. Then, as the two entered the yard, Broderick slowed abruptly, holding Boegus back also.

"What you spotted?" whispered Boegus, noting the uncomfortable look on the captain's face.

"It's him," replied Broderick weakly.

"Who's him?" asked Boegus, noting there were several on the front porch.

Finally, Boegus' eyes grew wide as he spotted the old, white-bearded fellow rocking in a wooden chair on the far side of the porch.

"Basil," he said weakly. "What'll we do?"

"Just keep coming," spoke the old fellow loudly as he slowly stood from the chair, eying the two.

A bit stooped, and well under six feet tall, the old elf looked almost frail compared to the others as he slowly worked his way through them. The breeze gently blew his thinning white hair from his face as he stepped down the porch steps. Dressed in a beige robe trimmed in crimson, he leaned upon a staff that looked older than he was. But, all in all, he still looked every bit a wizard.

"Find what you've been looking for?" he asked.

His pale, blue eyes sparkled with clarity uncommon for his age as he searched the dwarves' expressions for a clue most others would miss.

Noting Feathersmore and the other elves were grinning, Broderick replied, "Yes . . . and no Sir."

Knowing that Old Basil wasn't the most patient of the Alvis family, Boegus grimaced, and then rubbed his face briskly.

Little by little, a smile formed on the face of the old wizard as a young, sandy-haired lad eased close to his Right side.

"What to do?" asked the Wizard Basil as he looked down at the young gnome.

"They want the same thing," said Yenwolk. "I think it's like some kind of game to them."

"Game..." The old one mused the situation as he watched to two dwarves squirm. He looked back at Feathersmore and said, "Join us." Then, turning back to Yenwolk, he said, "Let me have what they seek."

The wizard took the scale from the lad and held it in his open hand in front of them. "This was presented to the lad by the 'Watcher' himself. This was to prove to others of his existence," he explained. "Pandahar, or the

Pan as my son is so fond of calling him, is under a charge to protect the lad until he becomes of age." His face then clouded up in anger as he pointed a crooked finger at Feathersmore, and then slowly swung it toward Broderick. "You two would distract him from that with your pointless, little pursuit," he grumbled.

Then, as the two watched, the scale in his hind split in twain.

"You may take you each a piece," he instructed. "You now have two choices. I will set my dragon, Doppelganger, between the Cutoff and the Oxbow Lake. If either of you get past him and are still able to hold the object which I give you, you will have won the prize you seek."

"That could be a great deal of trouble," whispered Boegus as Feathersmore slowly nodded.

"We know your red dragon," said Broderick. "He doesn't play well with others I think. May we know the other choice?"

The old wizard nodded with, "Give what you would have won to the Stonesmith family. They can use it for the lad." he answered without hesitation.

"Auugh!" groaned Broderick as he turned and looked toward Belinda's garden.

"Unfair, Broderick?" asked Basil. "Perhaps you would like to play with my dragon on your way back to the lake."

The old wizard held the scale halves a bit closer to the dwarf. But, with the thought of what Doppelganger had done in the past when Basil was young, Broderick slowly faced the old wizard, and then asked, "Would a price of silver do as well?"

"Well?" Old Basil looked down at Yenwolk. "What do you think?"

"Not sure, Sir," responded Yen. "I wouldn't want to spoil a friendship with the elves or the dwarves."

"Well put, my puzzling, young friend," responded Basil. Then, as he looked back up at the two, he added, "My 'game' is not of the lad's doing and I don't expect any hard feelings toward him to arise out of this situation. How does three, one-ounce ingots sound?"

"Auugh!" complained Broderick again as he watched Feathersmore and the other elves quickly search their pockets. Then, looking at the scale pieces still held out in the old wizard's hand, he slowly took out his pouch, fished out the required amount, and then handed it to the young gnome.

"Take it," encouraged Basil, noting that Yen was hesitating. "A wizard never refuses a rightful gratuity. These two would have sport with a creature that clearly had his forehands full already. But, all in all, they have learned a most valuable lesson--never vex a wizard, especially one from the Whitestone Castle."

Sixth Offering:
Spotter: A True Story

U.S.A.F. Jargon:
GATOR...Ground to Air—Transmit Or Receive
IFF... Identification—Friend or Foe (Code supplied by remote GATOR site to help identify crafts in the air)
Boot... Heavy rubber shield used to block outside light from radarscope
BAR... Browning Automatic Rifle
Radron... Radar Squadron
NCOIC... Non-Commissioned Officer In Charge
UFO... Unidentified Flying Object
Squawking... Painting or displaying an IFF code on the scope to signify a friendly contact
Boot. . .Heavy, hard rubber shield over the radar scope.

The 609th Radar Squadron had been, to most folks, a pleasant place to serve or work out your enlistment. It was about ten miles south-southwest of Eufaula, Alabama and in a pristine woods that most hunters could only dream of. In the Summer days of 1967, it gave most of us a new meaning of the term UFO. . . .

Bill Grube, a tall, dark-haired young sergeant opened the door of the 609th Radar Squadron's Search lounge and looked across two hangar bays toward the security door on the far side of the building. "Are you going or not?" he said to his friend now standing close to the door.

The Texan eyed a brown-haired, Tennessee boy who was now holding the security door open. His concentration was on something other than what was inside the hangar bays.

"Want anything from the chow hall before we start

the game?" asked Rick Williamson as he looked back at the Texan.

"No, for heaven's sake. I'm about to bust out of these pants already. Five more pounds and I'll have to order a whole new set of uniforms. Shut that door and loosen the relay on the alarm panel. If Lt. Isaco tries to sneak in, he'll set the wrong code alarm off. He's the only one who objects to our little pinochle games."

"Very well," agreed the Tennessee boy. He reached inside the metal cover on the door and loosened the small, plug-in relay. "It's set," added the sergeant through a grin. "We've been doing this for three months now and he hasn't caught on yet." Rick walked briskly toward the break room and added, "Who's sitting in on the game tonight, Grube?"

"Bill Anderson and Hank Shoultz. They're through with their work also on both height finders. And by the way, it's already Friday and if we don't catch up by Sunday night, our team will have to buy the pizza again."

Rick shook his head as he entered the break room. "This pinochle stuff is gonna break me yet," he added, looking at Hank already dealing out the cards.

Then, before Rick could sit down, the claxon alarm went off above the main scope.

"Dogonnet!" exclaimed Hank as he plopped the remainder of the cards on the table. "Just when I was getting comfortable."

The tall, thin, Georgia boy across from him drug his self out of his padded lounge chair and reluctantly followed Rick and Hank from the lounge and into the main hangar bay. Bill Anderson, or Andy as he was called, seldom worried about a thing. Being a devout Christian, the blond-haired boy had the utmost confidence in things working out for the good.

"I'll check the output gauges on Able channel, Rick," said Bill as he headed toward the main control panel. "They might be a little low and this will be an easy fix."

"I'll get the master scope," added Rick. "I'll bet something out there's not squawking."

"Just peachy," complained Hank, "That'll bring the Old Man up here for sure."

Rick ran straight for the master scope with his hands over his ears. "Turn off that blame thing. I can't hear myself think!" he shouted.

Andy headed for the reset button in the breaker room at a dead run. The ahh-oo-gah quickly ceased.

"Forget it, Hank!" shouted Rick, looking like his face was glued to the boot of the master scope. "We've got another one low in from the south again." Rick looked up from the scope. "Hank, inform Height Finder number two. Get us a fix and speed on this thing."

Hank ran into the office and punched up Baker Height Finder on the loud speaker.

"Still there?" asked Andy as he ran back from the breaker room.

Rick nodded with, "and coming in fast!"

"Tell 'em about it, Rick! They're on the main speaker!" said Hank loudly as he burst out of the office

"Hello, Height," said Rick loudly.

"Ready and willing," said the voice on the speaker.

"Bogie from the south. Third blip. She's about a one-seventy-five out and coming straight for us."

"Crank it around due south!" shouted a voice in the background.

"We've got it," said another.

"Hello, Search," the speaker blared out again.

"Give me something quick," said Rick

"Four hundred feet and close to Mach two,"

"Damn!" said Hank loudly. "Let me see."

Rick moved back from the master scope and looked at Andy. "Inform Montgomery Field for verification and support and then get the Old Man on the phone quick. Alert GATOR and tell whoever's down the hill there that this is no drill." Rick then turned to Grube and said, "Call Eastman at the AP shack and tell them to wake up the Sac team and have them stand by."

"One-fifty out and running like a bat out of Hell!" exclaimed Hank. He looked up from the boot and then added, "He's still coming straight for us."

Just then, Andy came bursting out of the office.

"I've got GATOR armed. They're looking."

"Sweet Jesus! I forgot," exclaimed Rick as he looked at Andy. "Billy Weeks is on duty at GATOR tonight. He's the only one of us who has actually got a good look at this thing last time."

"Lord," said Andy weakly. "Bullwinkle's armed? The last one scared him so bad he came down from his post and locked himself in the building."

Rick grabbed Andy, spun him around, and pushed him back toward the office. "Call the AP shack on the gate. Have them tell the SAC team that Bull is down there with a BAR and for God's sake don't run in on him."

"One hundred miles out!" shouted Hank. "It ain't waitin' for nobody."

"Just great," complained Rick. "Major McKenzie will miss this one also."

"He's gonna be pissed," quipped Hank without looking up.

Just then, Andy stuck his head out of the office and said, "Montgomery's up. We've got three Phantoms blowin' and goin' and heading our way."

"The SAC team's been warned," said Grube as he snatched a pair of field glasses from the coat rack and then ran for the security door.

"Good idea," said Rick. He handed Hank another pair and said, "I've got the main scope. Take these to the roof. If that thing ducks out on us again, perhaps you can spot where it goes down."

"Got it," said Hank as he grabbed a radio from the pegboard next to the office door. "If he goes down I'll buzz you," he added as he ran for the roof ladder in the far corner of the second bay.

Rick quickly checked the scope and then looked right back up at Grube on the door. "Fifty miles out!" he shouted toward the Texan. "Look for it! Look for it! It's gonna be right on top of us before you know it."

When Grube propped the security door open he turned toward Rick. "I can see the lights of Cookie's Pontiac. The goat's up but it ain't rollin'," he added loudly.

"Nuts!" exclaimed Rick as he looked back into the boot of the master scope. "Well under fifty now, people and still smokin'."

"Hello, Search," came a voice blaring over the speaker again.

"Search here," answered Rick.

"Last paint on bogie showed five miles out at one-hundred-eighty feet."

"Damn!" shouted Rick as he looked up toward Grube from the main scope. "That Height Finder paints five to our one. That sap sucker's under signal again." Rick then grabbed his walkie-talkie. "Come in, Hank," he said loudly.

"Still here. Come back," said Hank.

"Looks like the show's over, Hank. Did you see anything?"

"Got a glimpse of something bright through top of the trees but couldn't tell much. Don't see anything right now."

"Come on down, Hank. Height's gonna watch that area for us a bit."

"Roger. I'm on my way."

"Lost him again," said Rick as he looked back at Grube at the door nodding his head. "The Old Man's gonna be pissed."

Grube then spun around to see the chief cook's yellow GTO slide up with three other armed riflemen. Major McKenzie did much the same from the other direction in his red Galaxy 500. They ended up almost nose-to-nose in front of Grube.

"What do we have, Grube?" asked the Commander of the base.

Bill shrugged his shoulders. "I'm afraid we lost it again, sir,"

The Commander shook his head slowly as he walked past Grube and toward the main scope. It was easy to see that these little events were becoming personal challenges to him. He wanted desperately to get a closer look at the strange, glowing object that had flown circles around them for several months now. Most of the time, it wouldn't come closer than five miles or so and then just disappear. Three weeks ago, the 'Billy Weeks Incident' made it even more personal-one of his men had actually been put in a possible 'Harms Way' situation. According to Billy, the ship was about the size of a Corvette, glowed silver, and was shaped like an almond. If that wasn't enough, it made little sound, except for a slight static-like buzz.

"We lost it again?" asked the Major as he walked up to the main scope.

"Yes sir," answered Rick. "One to two miles out to the south—much like most of the others."

"It didn't go up," added Hank as he joined them. "I was on the roof with field glasses. I could see it through the trees at times, but it was very low--perhaps thirty feet or so. I believe it's down there in the woods right now.

The major spun around and looked at Andy. "Get on the horn!" he ordered, "Inform Montgomery Field. Advise them it's down a mile or so due south of us."

"Lordy!" exclaimed Cookie as he ran in with his hands over his ears.

It quickly became apparent that support had arrived when the roar of the Phantoms quickly shook the huge metal building.

"Sounded like the fighters flew straight through the hangars!" grumbled Cookie, Chief Sergeant in charge of the Chow Hall.

Major McKenzie flung his cap down on the polished concrete floor. "These blasted things are making us look like buffoons!" he exclaimed. "We have to do something different, boys."

"It's time to think outside the box," said Grube as he walked up to the Major.

The Major picked up his cap, slowly sat down on the edge of the scope's console, and then looked at the young sergeant. "Just how do we go about that?" he asked, squinting his eyes at the Texan.

"Just like we hunt, Major," said Sergeant Grube. "Rick and I, along with three others, know and have hunted these woods. We need to look for it. There's an abandoned fire tower just southeast of here. It's in pretty good shape and would offer a perfect view for us. Perhaps we can spot where the next one lands."

The Major cocked his head, squinted his eyes, and then replied, "I'm not going to ask how you know that, but I'll get authorization from the Forestry Service to use the tower. You pick out three other men who know these woods and man that thing day and night until I tell you different." The CO then paused, ran his fingers through his salt and pepper hair, and then looked back at Grube. "One other thing," he added. "This little plan of ours never happened. On paper, you and the others will be at your normal posts. Take what you need in the way of supplies, especially the short wave unit. Don't answer a thing or break the silence unless completely necessary. Your call ID will be Spotter. When you hear that, I want someone in that tower to answer ASAP. Is that clear?"

"Yes sir," replied Sergeant Grube.

"We don't want to get our butts in a sling over this, Bill," added McKenzie. "Above all, there will be no weapons issued to any of you."

"I understand, Major," said Sergeant Grube. "The others will as well. I'll get Rick and Hank here, and Raymond House at the Baker Height Unit. They know these woods better than anyone else I know."

"Good," replied McKenzie through a smile. "Make me a map with grids and sectors. I want something good enough for Montgomery Field to use when this thing comes calling again."

* * *

Time and pinochle games passed without so much as a shooting star for ten days. Then, on a Tuesday morning, Raymond House, then the Spotter Team's link to the Search Unit, busied himself by checking the readings of the FPS-24 Search Unit's back up Transmitter. When he heard the security door open, he looked around the cabinet to see Hank walk in, fidgeting with his walkie-talkie.

House shut the door of the cabinet and walked quickly toward him. "What are you doing here?" he asked. "You're supposed to be in the tower now."

"Would've called but this blame thing keeps going

in and out," grumbled Hank. "I've never heard static quite like this before," said Hank as he continued to adjust the unit. "Besides, a forest ranger told me to vacate the place." Hank then handed House a piece of paper and added, "Here's his name."

"Thomas Smith?" asked House. "Put that radio on the table by the pegboard and get yourself a fresh one with a good supply of batteries. I'm going to check this out with the Old Man right now."

As Hank swapped out the radio and searched for batteries, he watched House through the big window that overlooked both Able and Baker bays from the office. When House's expression grew from inquisitive to surprised, Hank walked quickly back to the office door.

"Get back to that tower," said House as he burst out of the office. "McKenzie checked with the Forestry Service. There is no Thomas Smith assigned here or anywhere else in Alabama."

"Then, who was he?" asked Hank.

"How the Devil should I know?" grumbled House. "Just get back there and monitor that radio. If that static starts again, change to channel five, buzz me and say you've went to plan 'B'. I'll go to that channel immediately."

"No problem," said Hank as he ran for the security door.

* * *

Shortly after receiving the news of the mysterious forest ranger, Sergeants Bill Grube and Rick Williamson decided to spend the rest of the day, and possibly the night, with Hank at the tower. With a cooler of supplies and a change of clothes, they met their friend at the tower around noon. Now, armed with blankets, pillows, and a stick of rag bologna, they awaited the possible return of the one who evicted Hank.

* * *

The hard, wooden floor shook beneath Rick, jarring him awake. He could see it was now dark, as well as Hank rolled up in one of the blankets not more than three feet from him. All the windows were propped open and the cool night air was a welcomed treat opposed to the hot muggy day before. When the floor trembled again, Rick slowly sat up.

"Feel that," whispered Grube, who was standing watch at the southern-most windows.

Rick nodded, threw back the blanket, and then walked to the windows on the east side.

"Rick," whispered the Texan.

Rick turned to see him lay his hand on one of the windowsills.

Following his lead, Rick put his hand on the sill in front of him. It was vibrating—not like what woke him up, but vibrating none-the-less.

"What the Devil is it?" whispered Rick. "I can feel—"

"Come in, Spotter. This is House. Over," blared out the radio.

"Turn that damned thing down quick," said Grube, sending Rick scrambling for the short wave unit.

"What the..." said Hank as he clawed from under his blanket.

"Shhh," hissed Rick as he picked up the radio. "Rick here," he answered softly as he added, "We've got a situation."

"You bet you have, replied House. "Height has just spotted a bogie out of nowhere. Didn't fly in at all. It just popped up right where the fighters last looked for it. It's now down again in the same place just south of you—sector D-17."

"Get the light," said Rick to Hank as he opened the map.

"Spotter, come in," squawked the radio again.

"Rick here,"

"Harriers dispatched on a sit and watch basis. Watch for them just east of that sector."

"What direction, Rick?" asked Grube.

"South-southeast and on the ground."

"Let's go," said Hank as he threw back his blanket and pulled out a forty-five automatic.

"Great Cesar's ghost!" exclaimed Grube as quiet as his excitement would allow. "Why'd you bring that thing? The Old Man said no weapons. He'll have a cow if he finds out one of us has a weapon."

"I can see it now," added Rick. "World class incident at the 609th Radron causes Commander to loose pension."

Hank rolled his eyes as he tucked the pistol back under the blanket. "I'll leave it here," he added reluctantly. "But I'm not a bit pleased with that idea."

"Duly noted," said Grube as he opened the trap door to the stairs.

"Straight south," replied Rick. As he and Hank followed the Texan, Rick added, "About a mile or so, we'll come to a little valley. That's Pea Creek. We'll then head almost east. D-17 shouldn't be that far."

Half running, half jogging, the Spotters pushed their way through scrub pines, wild hedge, and dewberry brambles until they came to the little, eight-mile valley.

"We'll go left here," said Rick as they edged down the leafy slope to the bottom.

"For Pete's sake," whispered Grube, "be as quiet as possible. We're about half a mile from it and we don't want to spook them."

"Them?" echoed Hank as he stepped up closer to Grube.

"Whoever flies that thing, Hank," answered the Texan.

"Or whatever," added Hank uncomfortably.

About a mile down the creek, Rick slowed and crouched down next to a willow oak, motioning for them to do the same.

"What is it?" whispered Hank as he and Grube knelt by the brown-haired Tennessee boy.

Rick pointed up ahead of them toward a narrow part of the valley that made a blind turn to the south.

"Something's glowing just around that hill. It's not very bright, but it's there none-the-less."

"So is that vibration," whispered Hank. "Feel of this tree."

Rick put his ear against the trunk tree and smiled. "Never heard an oak tree hum," he quipped. He then looked at Hank and replied quietly, "A little closer if you please."

Hank rolled his eyes toward Grube and mumbled, "Three airmen abducted by aliens in Alabama turn up in North Dakota—naked and abused."

"Will you quit," said Grube, laughing quietly. "Just keep your eyes open."

"Wait for me," suggested Hank, "and I'll go back for the pistol."

"Definitely not," snapped Grube. "Just keep close."

After another fifty yards or so, Rick stopped the group again at the base of a huge, white oak and knelt behind one of its bark-covered roots.

"I see 'em," whispered Grube as the two crowded up behind Rick.

Standing atop the hill that separated them from whatever was making the dim light were two distinct silhouettes.

"Lord Almighty," said Hank weakly. "I see 'em also —two of 'em and not much more than three feet tall."

"What's on their heads?" whispered Grube.

"I'm afraid that is their head," answered Rick.

Hank eased passed Grube a bit and stopped, kneeling in the leaves. "You've got to be kiddin'."

The silhouette above their neck was shaped like a hamburger bun and almost as wide as its shoulders. To describe them as stick men wouldn't be far from the truth. At times, for some strange reason, you could see light being reflected from their mirror-like eyes on the top end of their 'heads'.

"Ohhh, this is too good," said Grube. As he slowly backed away he added, "You two stay here and I'll get behind them."

"Are you crazy!" exclaimed Hank.

"Shhh!" hissed Rick. "One more noise like that and we'll lose our chance for sure."

"Stay here, girls," quipped Grube as he started crawling up the bank. "Give me a minute or two. I'm gonna get behind them."

After about five minutes, Rick started to ease from the tree for a better look, but was pulled back behind the root.

"I wouldn't go just yet," whispered Hank as he pointed toward the hill.

As Rick crouched back down again, he noticed the two figures were holding something that glowed.

"What are they doing?" asked Hank weakly as dull, orange balls floated from their hands.

One of the tennis ball sized objects went northwest where Grube was headed and the other drifted down the hill and then headed up the creek toward them.

"Behind these roots," said Rick. "Get as close to them as you can."

The orb floated lazily up the creek about ten feet off the ground. When it neared them, it slowed slightly, but then continued on up the valley.

"What's with this hum," whispered Hank as he peeped over a bark-covered root at Rick.

Rick looked back at Hank to see him with his ear pressed against the root.

"You don't have to do that," whispered Rick. "I can hear it, and it's getting louder."

"Duck!" snapped Hank.

Taking good advice, Rick hugged the root once more as the glowing ball shot back up the creek toward the hill and the aliens.

"Oh my God," said Hank weakly. He pointed toward the top of the hill and then added, "They've got him."

As Rick peeped back over the root of the oak, he could see that the strange silhouettes were gone, but there was another that took their place. This one was much taller—six-foot-four to be exact.

"They've got Grube," said Rick just above a whisper.

"That's just great," complained Hank. "What now?"

"Well, it's not checkmate yet," answered Rick. "Call it in. The Harriers are just a spit away from us."

As Hank fumbled in the dark for the radio, the audible humming ceased as the glow behind the hill increased dramatically.

"Something's happening," said Hank as he gripped the radio like a baseball bat.

As they both watched the Texan's silhouette, the distinct hissing sound of the Harriers filled the air almost above them. Their distinct, green and blue lights circled cautiously above the glowing object now rising from the ground. Even more distinctive now was the static charges that were being released from the craft to the trees as it brushed their limbs.

Pine needles, bark, and small limbs filled the air as the two airmen ran toward the hill and their friend, still standing there stone still. When they started up toward Grube, Rick paused to check above them. The mysterious craft was now clearly above the trees—pausing for a moment as if observing the two fighters. Then, before you could say Jumpin' Jack Flash, it went straight up between the Harriers. The wash created by that maneuver, not only stirred even the leaves and limbs around them, but also caused both fighters to take evasive maneuvers.

"Damn it!" exclaimed Hank as he buried his face in his hands. "My eyes are full of dust, Rick! Go and help Grube!"

With the exhaust screaming from the two fighters as they gave chase, Rick quickly ran up the hill and toward the Texan. He was standing like a cigar store Indian, staring across the valley at who knows what.

"Bill," said Rick as he tapped the man's left forearm.

Grube blinked, but still didn't look at anything in particular.

"Grube!" shouted Rick. He took hold of his arm and added, "Are you all right?"

Grube slowly looked up toward the noise the Harriers were making and then back down at Rick. "How did I get here?" he asked as he slowly rubbed his eyes.

"You don't know?" asked Hank as he walked up behind Rick. "You big Texan," he added with a sigh of relief, "you could of at least grabbed one of 'em."

Grube tried to smile, but the expression on his face didn't quite make it. Instead, he just slowly shook his head with, "The last clear thing I remember was coming face to face with some kind of glowing ball," he explained. "Oh, and I think Hank's Ranger friend, Thomas Smith, was there with the strangest people. He called them the Baskins." Grube then stopped talking and grew wide-eyed as if remembering something important.

"Go ahead!" said Rick. "We're still here and listening."

"There's another!" he exclaimed as he wheeled around and started back down the hill.

"Another what?" asked Rick as he and Hank followed as close as they could.

"Forget another," quipped Hank. "I'm still working on that Baskins part."

"Little People," answered Grube as he stopped abruptly.

When Rick and Hank eased up by him, they could immediately see what the Texan was referring to. Another craft lay nestled in the mouth of a leaf-filled gully almost below them. It was the color of a black olive and just as shiny. Looking about eighteen feet long and four feet tall at its tallest point, it was shaped just like a peach seed.

Rick eased around Hank and approached the ship.

"What are you doing?" asked Hank.

"Working on bragging rights," replied Rick as he continued.

"Good then," quipped Hank. "I'll stay right here and work on that Baskin thing."

Keeping his eyes on Rick, Grube replied, "They're just weird little people, Rick. They sound like Munchkins and called us too nosy and unpredictable."

Rick eased up to the strange looking object like it was alive and might jump at him at any moment. "This thing has no seams, fellas," he said softly as if fearful of waking it. "It doesn't feel like metal either; it's warm and supple...like something living."

Rick then stumbled back and fell to the ground. "It shocked me," he said as he quickly regained his feet.

The ships surface then started to pulsate with such intensity, they could feel it hum through the ground beneath their feet. Rick slowly backed from the strange craft for now it had started to glow very dimly. Then, as the glow intensified, it started producing bright bands of vertical rings that moved slowly over it from what looked to be its nose to its tail.

"What's it doing?" said Rick as he kept backing from the mysterious looking craft.

"I'll tell you in a minute or two," said Grube.

Rick turned to see both Hank and Grube scrambling away from the creek bed.

Suddenly, I feel quite out of place, thought Rick. He quickly turned and raced after them.

"Get the Old Man on the horn!" said Grube to Hank as they both stopped and looked back at Rick run up beside them.

"And do what?" interrupted Rick as he joined them. "Come down here and help us watch? That strange light display on the ship looked like a warning to me."

"Exactly," added Hank as he pulled the two airmen toward the far side of a huge white oak.

Once on the other side, Hank stopped. "Hear that?" he said softly. "It's like bacon sizzling in a hot skillet."

"That's new?" quipped Grube.

With the edge of the small creek bed still in sight, the temptation was just too great for the Texan. He eased toward it and away from the other two.

"There you go again," said Hank, glancing at Rick. "You're gonna loose your head when that thing goes off."

Paying no regard to the warning, Hank peeked over the hill. "Oh, guys," he said melodically, "come see this."

Rick and Hank hurried up beside Grube and watched as the ship began to do something very strange. It could only be described as ridding itself of this world. Glowing at first on its topmost part, it began to do what only be described as melting--crackling and bubbling like fish filet dropped into hot oil. This continued until it was completely gone, even unto its bottom-most part. All that was left was a patch of black material resembling pea gravel.

"I don't believe it!" said Grube, as he smacked a sapling next to him with his fist. "We had it right here with us!"

Rick shook his head as they looked at the granules in the blackened spot. "I don't believe we ever had it," he added. “Nor do I believe we will in my lifetime.”

“Hank turned and looked at Rick. “You’re ranking man here,” he said. “What do you think we should put in our report? McKenzie’s gonna ask a million questions.”

“We’ll take some of those little, black balls with us and tell the truth,” replied Rick with a grin. “Let him pick out what he wants to believe.”

“Are you kidding?” said Grube angrily. “The truth dies here—right here in the 609th. When they come from Montgomery Field to debrief us, they’ll decide what the truth will be and I’ll guarantee the both of you, we probably won’t be able to recognize it at all.”

Hank then turned and ran down toward the blackened silhouette in the leaves. The light from his flashlight danced on the dark, green crystals that lay in front of him.

“Good Lord,” said Grube, just above a whisper, “he’s snapped. He’s completely out of character.”

Rick laughed as the two walked up to the kneeling figure. “They’re not ashes?” he asked.

“Not at all,” replied Hank as he held out a handful toward the two. “They’re cool and almost perfectly round. I thought they were black cinders, but they look kind of like emeralds, dark and green.”

“My word,” said Rick as Hank poured the pea-sized crystals in his hands. “Before I die,” Rick added softly, “I would like to know what we just saw, who the Baskins are, and where they come from.”

“Me also,” said Grube as he also scooped up a hand full of the dark green objects. “At least one of ‘em looked like us, and seemed to be friendly enough.” As the three turned and walked from the remnants of the craft he added, “I can only surmise they judge our world just the opposite.”

Epilog:

This short story was inspired by actual events that took place in the Summer of 1967 both in and around the 609th Radron near Eufaula, Alabama. Coupled with the later investigative reports of Dan Rather, this work offers a both clear and descriptive testimony to the fact that we are not alone. The last paragraph was the consensus of our group when the 609th Radar Site was closed later that year. Although it is inactive, it is still there and guarded on Hangar Road just ten miles south of Eufaula. To this date, I am still wondering...

Printed in the USA
CPSIA information can be obtained
at www.ICGtesting.com
LVHW012019300124
770046LV00012B/375

9 798868 904813